Feast

Bisma Tirmizi has been a weathered storyteller for twenty-seven years, first as an employee at The Herald Group of Publications for over six years in the capacity of a sub-editor, and then as a freelance journalist. She has penned over five hundred articles and has been published in *Dawn, The News, The Express Tribune* and *Buzzfeed* amongst many others. Her musings over a cup of tea almost always find their way to be the written word, either in the form of an article, story, commentary and now a book.

She has been writing Food Stories for dawn.com for over four years, and has been enjoying food forever. This is her debut novel, sketching an elemental love story between us and our unique, nurturing and, at times, obsessive relationship with food, and the social relationships surrounding it. She lives in Las Vegas, United States.

Praise for the book

Evocative, engaging and a feast in itself, this book traces the importance of our regional cuisines and ties them with memory, emotion and familial bonds. Bisma's narrative presents painstakingly collated recipes of our favourite food items but takes us beyond the culinary senses into more complex territories of self-discovery, time travel and search for fulfillment. Above all, it is also a testament to how food connects and remains an unappreciated binding force in a region bruised by never-ending conflict.

—Raza Rumi, author, journalist and Editor, *Daily Times*

A love story goes to the heart. Good food tickles the palate. Combined, they touch the soul. Peppered with recipes and stories of how they evolved, the delicacy that emerges is a 'culinary romance' that is irresistible. Bisma Tirmizi is outstanding here!

—Zubeida Mustafa, Winner of Lifetime Achievement Award, International Women Media Foundation, Former Assistant Editor, *Dawn*

You need to be a dedicated Biryani-foodie to go through this imaginative chronicle.

—Bapsi Sidhwa, Author

A fascinating account of life and cuisine in the subcontinent, Bisma's first book is a welcome diversion from the dark times we live in.

— Ayesha Azfar, Assistant Editor, *Dawn*

Feast

With a Taste of
Amir Khusro

Bisma

BISMA TIRMIZI

Dear Pam

Shine on!

RUPA

Published by
Rupa Publications India Pvt. Ltd 2017
7/16, Ansari Road, Daryaganj
New Delhi 110002

Sales Centres:
Allahabad Bengaluru Chennai
Hyderabad Jaipur Kathmandu
Kolkata Mumbai

ISBN: 978-81-291-4901-5

First impression 2017

10 9 8 7 6 5 4 3 2 1

The moral right of the author has been asserted.

Printed at Thomson Press India Ltd., Faridabad

For my parents, Naheed and Javed,
nothing without you.
My Nani, Jamila Khatoon,
a storyteller extraordinaire.
My Dadi, Amna Khatoon,
in death, larger than life.

Contents

Recipes

Prologue

Gulnaar Jahan, cousin of Mughal Emperor Zaheer-ud-din Babur, sat pining for her homeland, Istilaf. She would still be there if Babur had not won the Battle of Panipat in 1526.

North of Kabul, Istilaf, nestled between the glorious ranges of the Hindu Kush on the one side and the gardens and fruit-laden orchards of the Shumaili Plains on the other, was heaven. Besides, as the oldest of five sisters, Gulnaar Jahan had been promised in marriage to the handsome Khurram Barani from Bulandshar. Her nuptials were to be solemnized in a few days, with the approval of Babur. But tragedy had struck, and soon thereafter her father had received a summons from Babur. Having dispatched the opposition gathered at Panipat in 1526, the Emperor had returned from the battlefield and demanded that his extended family migrate to Hindustan to live out their years with him. Ah, the arrogance of the powerful, and the lives they destroy to please their ego.

And so, late in the summer of 1528, a caravan had set out from Istilaf and ended up on the dusty plains of the Indus. Gulnaar's father, a proud Timurid, loyal advisor and paternal uncle to Babur had felt a compelling need to stay on in Hindustan, even after Babur's untimely death in the year 1530. Hence, Gulnaar was forced to part ways with Istilaf, much like her ill-fated romance with Khurram.

Gulnaar and Khurram's love story was as passionate as it was short. His brother tragically died and the ancient custom of '*chadaar charhana*', where the unmarried brother-in-law married the widowed sister-in-law, came into play. Those were times when traditions and customs took precedence over faith, much as they do today. And so, though betrothed to Gulnaar, the duty-bound Khurram was married off to his young widowed sister-in-law. He offered to marry Gulnaar at the same time, but heartbroken, she refused.

> *Chaos existed then, as it does today,*
> *Spirituality flourished, as it does today,*
> *Peace was elusive, as it is today,*
> *Love hung in the balance, as it does today,*
> *And I, Feast, nurtured all of the beasts and humanity, then, as*
> *I still do today.*

Bulandshar, winter 1555

Memories of lost love were still potent and alive and twenty-four years later, on the eve of her son's marriage, Gulnaar was still wondering why fate had torn her and Khurram apart. And then, she mused, so that her three younger sons from her current marriage could have been born, thus ensuring the continuity in lineage of her husband's family, since her husband was the only surviving son in his family.

Gulnaar's eldest son married the daughter of Muhammad Khan Balouch. Khan Balouch had marched with Humayun's troops, when the second Mughal Emperor had arrived in Hindustan to reclaim his throne as the heir to Babur's dynasty. The proud tribal leader claimed allegiance to the Emperor and had lavishly welcomed the Emperor's great aunts—for Gulnaar Jahan always travelled with her four sisters, much like the seven Saiyyed sisters she claimed ancestry from.

In return for Khan Balouch's support, and that of his tribe during the bloody wars that had ensued, he had been granted large and fertile lands by the Emperor. The wedding was lavish, as matched Khan Balouch's stature.

Marriage, birth and death, Gulnaar pondered, were controlled by the heavens, for these were the only real determinants of a man's permanent pathway. She got up and strolled to the bridal chamber. There, laid out were large platters of rice, raisin and pomegranate-stuffed lamb, marinated in salt.

The alluring wafts of saffron took Gulnaar further back—to when her wedding preparations had begun in full swing and nobody knew that she and Khurram secretly met in her chambers. She reminisced about the passion that Khurram's touch had awakened in her and the fervour of its ultimate culmination. She smiled wistfully, at the almost palpable memory of the textured lamb, infused with the aroma of pomegranate melting in her mouth as she fed a tender bite to Khurram. He held her hand, and her gaze, the plate of the effervescent lamb pulao forgotten. She had snapped her fingers playfully wanting to break his gaze, and then picked up a morsel from the plate of pulao and offered it to him with her henna-decorated hand.

He had kissed her fingers tenderly and closed his eyes. She had too, breathing in the aroma of the fragrant pulao, and somehow sealing in the scent with the moment. A way to a man's heart was through nurturing and love, and a woman feeding a man delicious food with her hand was considered the most sensuous form of nurturing. Countless were the love stories solemnized into weddings and unions, where the sensuous pulao had played a role in bringing a man and a woman together. She had, even then, thanked her ancestors for passing on the tradition of pulao-making from generation to generation.

In that room with Khurram, the sweetness in the air was not only of the raisins plumped inside the lamb, but also of his playful stroking of her hair and skin. She remembered snugging her shawl around her shoulders, and swaying nymph-like to the distant sound of *dhol* playing host to '*Main to piya say naina lada aayi ray*', by the incomparable Amir Khusro, and playfully pushing Khurram's hand away, telling him he must leave. But the combination of lamb pulao, rice-stuffed whole lamb, and sweet milk seemed to have played havoc with Khurram's senses. She could either call out to her lady-in-waiting, in which case he would have to leave before she entered the chambers, or succumb to his charms. She chose the latter, seeking comfort in the knowledge that her *nikaah* was only a few days removed.

> *Main to piya say naina lada aayi ray,*
> *Ghar naari kanwari kahay so karay,*
> *Main to piya say naina lada aayi ray.*

If only she had known then what she knew now, she would have made another choice:

> *The choice of utmost pleasure,*
> *Laced in delight,*
> *A journey worth a thousand words,*
> *A legend, a tale so bright.*

Simla, 1943

Shireen sat at a picnic bench eating mutton pulao, Nandini Samra sat on her right and Sharmeena Barani on her left. The three-tier silver tiffin-box, packed with pulao, glistened in the late-morning sunlight that peeped through the lush foliage canopying the school grounds. Each grain of rice lay separate from the next, and the emanating aroma spread to the benches close by. Frenie Javat smelled pulao from across the aisle and signaled a thumbs up to Shireen.

Every Tuesday Shireen's mother made mutton pulao and sent it to school at lunch time, and every Tuesday the three girls sat together and two devoured the rice dish to the last grain.

As the three girls sat giggling, Sister Geraldine, one of the newer nuns at Convent of Jesus and Mary, Simla, stood observing them. *A beautiful trio they make, but caste and religion separates them from sharing a meal,* she thought.

The Convent of Jesus and Mary, a boarding school, stood amidst picturesque mountains and greenery. It was an orphanage-turned-boarding school and was famously called 'Chelsea'. It had been founded in 1864 by the nuns of Jesus and Mary, and soon flourished as a prestigious educational institution. Shireen had been enrolled there for a year and loved the stability and routine of boarding school. Her father was chief engineer in the Indian Railways and she travelled back and forth frequently to visit her family in Patiala and Ambala.

'By God, Shireen, your Amma makes the best pulao in the world,' said Sharmeena in her signature monotone.

'Yes, Amma makes the best pulao in the world, and there is a reason for it. The women in our family have been making mutton pulao for generations; I think from the time of Alexander the Great,' replied Shireen, almost wistfully, breathing in the subtle aroma of fennel.

'Alexander the Great! Are you Greek, Shireen?'

'No, she is crazy,' quipped Sharmeena, and they all fell about laughing.

But there was an element of truth in Nandini's question. Food travels through time and evolves through generations. Shireen's ancestors had migrated some 1,400 years ago from Arabia to Central Asia. Then in 1219, forced to flee Central Asia to escape the wrath of Chenghez Khan, they escaped to Afghanistan. Some more centuries later, their descendants had reached the plains of Eastern Punjab and became Punjabis thereafter. Their pulao recipe had travelled with them, and now, centuries later, Shireen's passion for Tuesdays with pulao had become a ritual.

Years later, the aromatic effervescence of fennel, coriander seeds and onions cooking in mutton broth would transport Shireen to her wonder years, a time when she thought that her dreams would live forever and all Tuesday lunches would be spent eating pulao, shami kabab and beetroot yogurt, sitting around a table of laughter and friends. Yes, those days were cut short but the joy of eating, cooking and butterfly kisses remained, to be passed on to generations to come.

Chapter 1

Karachi

Is Life an Elegant Pulao or a Fiery Biryani?

1984

Do I really look like Abida Parveen? Granted I sing like a powerhouse, but that's where the similarity must end.

I am Ayesha, thirteen, 145 lb, and a middle child sandwiched between two brothers. Did I mention I am short and fat, though Dadi insists it's baby fat? Today is the tenth of Muharram, the second day of the mourning, the day marking the martyrdom of Imam Hussain, the grandson of the Holy Prophet.

How does that translate into my realm besides the national mourning and the black sheets that drape the cinemas in the city?

It translates into mutton pulao, yes, mutton pulao!

Ammi's legendary annual homemade degh (cauldron, literally) of pulao is ready for distribution. Abbu says a prayer, setting a platter of rice in the centre of the dining table, a glass of water on its left and milk on its right. The pulao platter is mixed into the cauldron again so all may benefit from the said prayer.

Hence gluttony through pulao is now open for business, and pulao distribution begins to mark the great sacrifice by Prophet

Mohammed's grandson some 1,400 years ago at the grounds of Karbala.

Needless to say, I deeply care for the three categories of people, namely family, friends and the poor who will benefit from the prayer and the pulao, but not as much as I care about myself.

Today I will eat to my heart's content and there will be no counting of helpings, or portion size. My strategy is simple—step into the kitchen, ensure that our expert Bengali cook, Jalal, is nowhere in sight, serve a perfect plate of pulao, and slip into the verandah unnoticed. This strategy has worked well over the past three years, and today the household weather forecast predicts it will work well again, unless Nasreen Phuppo arrives unannounced and makes a commotion. She always comes unannounced (an extremely kosher and basic operational practice in Pakistan), wanting to meet her mother, my Dadi, who happens to live with us.

I sit in my rocking chair basking in the November sun with a plate of pulao at my service, and this is as good as it gets. The golden rice absorbs mutton stock for optimum flavour, each grain plumped to perfection, making the bite elegantly delicious. The essence of coriander seeds, onions, fennel and mutton boils to a perfect consommé, and the union is brought to perfection by the subtle hint of whole garam masalas playing hide and seek with my taste buds.

> *Little Miss Muffet, sat on a tuffet*
> *Eating her curds and whey*
> *Along came a spider*
> *Who sat down beside her*
> *And frightened Miss Muffet away*

Not!
Each bite takes me deeper into the world of calm, and mid-bite

I pause for a moment and breathe in the effervescence of fennel, eyes closed, savouring the moment and holding time captive for just a minute, and a fleeting déjà vu surrounds me.

∾

My family lives by the Arabian Sea in a single-storey home, an exactly thirteen minutes' walk from the beautiful coastline of Karachi. My room without a view is at the very back of the house, with a boring visual of a clothesline slung with hand washed whites. Dadi prefers the whites be hung in direct sunlight, and the colours under the ledge to avoid fading. It's hardly a bother since my favourite place to hangout is the front verandah and not my room.

The verandah is rectangular with three concrete whitewashed walls, two on the side and the back wall with a large French door that leads to the main house. The front of the verandah is made of beige lattice and is home to greens and flowers of all hues, bougainvillea vine topping the list. The flowering vine is abundant with flame orange and white, and since Ammi is very serious about her gardening, it is always in award-winning condition. We may not have water to bathe, given the water distribution efficiencies of the metropolis, but the grass is always greener on the other side, literally.

I am enthused by activity, people, the pleasant food smells coming from the neighbourhood, the sounds of the street, barking dogs and the chit-chat of the domestic traffic in and out of the house. I spend hours on end indulging in daydreams and mindless wonder, never getting bored of my verandah sit-ins.

My favourite spot is the far-left corner with the cushioned rocking chair and the daybed opposite it, where Dadi sits. The mattress covering the daybed and the cushion on the seat of the rocking chair are aqua blue, matching just as much as the two people who occupy them. In the centre of the verandah is the main seating area and the new cane furniture Ammi recently purchased from the cane market under Queens Road Bridge, next to the railway line leading to Cantt Station. She says the owner of the store claims that he is a direct descendant of Bahadur Shah Zafar, and would have been the Mughal Emperor today had the dynasty survived. The revelation is stunning, intriguing and humbling, a true story of prince to pauper, pathetic, but an interesting anecdote to be told when I invite my friends to sit on the cane sofa set.

The sofa, loveseat and two matching chairs are made with intricately woven cane, painted white and hosting lime green cushions. There are plants behind the seating area and a brick red rug by the front steps leading to the verandah. The coffee table has a large orange ceramic ashtray that is cleaned every day since Abbu enjoys an after-dinner pipe and, sometimes, a good Cuban cigar. The macramé plant hangers are Ammi's latest passion and are seen hanging in two opposite corners, my corner with the rocking chair and the one diagonal to it.

My verandah basks in the ethereal early morning light, and in my imagination that's how the light of heaven must appear. It almost always takes my breath away, and I find myself breathing to keep my heart beating. And I have the fleeting sensation, that if I hold on to my breath a little longer I could easily pass through a light similar to this and slip into the next dimension. But that can wait.

I frequently sit on my rocking chair, my favourite vantage point, and observe the world. People come and go, the gate bell rings to announce the coming of the newspaper boy, milkman, sweeper, laundryman, driver, gardener, junkyard man, water tanker and the list goes on. Interestingly, all and sundry, who pass by the verandah trellis, ask for a meal, either to consume or take home, and, surprisingly, there is always enough in our kitchen to go around. It could be leftover daal, cooked vegetables, naan, khichri, rice and fruit from the day before, or a full-fledged blessed cauldron of pulao to mark the day of mourning.

'This is your life in Karachi,' says Dadi, each time we have a philosophical discussion on life, people, borders and food. 'It could equally be your namesake's life in Lahore, Sargodha, Quetta, Peshawar, or in Delhi, Lucknow, Calcutta, Benaras and Bombay.[1] Another Ayesha might be sitting in a verandah in a village or a city, observing the same comings and goings, living through the same experiences; the Ayesha across the border could be chatting with her Dadi and doing the same.'

∽

Today Abbu visits his dear cousin, Tayajee Tyyab.

Tayajee Tyyab owns the Bismillah Biryani Centre on M.A. Jinnah Road leading to Quaid-e-Azam's mausoleum, and a very successful biryani venture in Karachi it is. Abbu insists on calling him a first cousin. Since Dada was an only child and my Dadi has just one brother who has no children, Abbu has no first cousins. However, I refrain from arguing his wisdom.

Bismillah Biryani sits on one of the main arteries of Karachi. My Dadi still refers to the road by its old name, Bunder Road, and I love calling it Bunder Road too, for monkey translates to 'bunder' in Urdu. The seaport is called 'bundergah', and since the road leads to the Karachi seaport, it was originally named Bunder Road. The thoroughfare is very busy, but slows down once the sun sets—which is the usual time of day we visit Bismillah Biryani. It is a large white structure on the main road close to Nishat Cinema,

---

[1]The cities of Mumbai and Kolkata are spelt as Bombay and Calcutta throughout this story, since the decision to change in their nomenclature was adopted after the fact and time, in which the book is situated.

busy as a bee and with severe parking issues.

The front wall is made of large casement French windows that extend a few inches above the floor. The panels are white as are the walls of the main dining hall inside. There are approximately thirty three-foot round tables with four chairs each in the main dining hall. Once rush hour begins, the turnaround at each table is fast. On the far right wall of the main entrance is a high breakfast bar with eight bar stools for singles to sit on and eat, on its right is the cash register facing the large red swinging door leading to the kitchen, and the ordering window with plantation shutters opening to the front of the main road.

A dozen wall fans, separated by large posters of national monuments of Pakistan, dot the walls. Six high ceiling fans—plus the fact that the front of the restaurant faces the West, inviting Karachi's evening cross-breeze—keep the temperatures pleasant, making it an ideal location to serve and devour biryani.

'Ammi, do you think Tayajee Tyyab will offer us biryani for dinner?'

Her disapproving glare screams Abida Parveen at me, reminding me that I pretty much run parallel with the Sufi singer's girth and voice extraordinaire. The stare leaves me disappointed, but disappointment has never stopped me from eating.

Tayajee Tyyab welcomes me with the warmth of an adopted relative, 'Ayesha is visiting us today! What do you want to drink, Fanta, 7UP with milk, chocolate, or some biscuits?'

He must think he can beat me at this game. No, no one beats me; I have acquired this chub with tenacity, persistence, patience and a whole lot of passion for delicious food. Biryani, I love thee. I wonder what Shakespeare would have written about biryani had he known it. I wonder if biryani was even around in the sixteenth century. Biryani, I crave thee, and as no one is interested in offering it to me, it's clear I'll have to muscle my way to it. With this thought I look to the left and spot Haji Sahib, Tayajee Tyyab's wingman, who nods a greeting and walks through the red swinging doors to the kitchen.

But before the biryani gets to me I'll give you a bit of background about rush hour at Bismillah Biryani.

∼

Rush hour at Bismillah Biryani

Haji Sahib stands in the middle of the kitchen and glances at the clock. Dinner time is upon the restaurant, there are unruly queues of people inside and a traffic jam of disarrayed cars outside, all looking for a sumptuous biryani dinner. The door swings open and with it the conundrum of demanding customers.

'Three plates ajrak biryani, with an extra helping of potatoes,' travels the voice of an ordering customer.

Haji Sahib picks up a copy of the new menu and shakes his head, amused; *Tyyab's son Yahya, a brilliant boy*, he thinks. It was Yahya's idea to revise the menu, renaming all biryanis on the menu with a colloquial tag to match the ethnicities they originated from.

MENU

Ajrak Biryani a.k.a. Sindhi Biryani
Luddan Biryani a.k.a. U.P. Biryani
Tug-ga Biryani a.k.a. Punjabi Biryani
Boria aur Bistaraa Biryani a.k.a. Bohri Biryani
Khan-e-khana Biryani aur Pulao a.k.a. Afghani Pulao
Hara Masala Biryani a.k.a. Punjab ki Haryalee

Deccan ke Dulhan Biryani a.k.a. Hyderabadi Dum Biryani
Bollywood Biryani a.k.a. Bombay Biryani
Banya Biryani a.k.a. Memoni Biryani
Mumtaz Mahal kay Ghar ki Biryani a.k.a. Ain-e-Akbari Biryani

At just nineteen, Yahya comes up with innovative ideas every day to improve the business, and almost every day Haji Sahib walks into an argument between father and son. Yahya wants to do an MBA, but Tayajee Tyyab wants him to pursue an MCom degree from the local Commerce College *and* join the family business part-time until he finishes college. Yahya wants to join Bismillah Biryani, but on his own terms. To Haji Sahib, at least, Yahya's insistence appears reasonable, zeal almost passionate, and loyalty towards the expansion of business, sincere. Haji thus often finds himself caught between father and son, and each day finds himself understanding Yahya's approach better.

'Haji Chacha, explain to Abba. An MBA will teach me the ropes of expanding the business, and from Bismillah Biryani I'll turn it to B. Bees, a new-age restaurant. We'll design a new logo, a new menu, a new approach—a biryani hangout place. You understand the word "cool"? I'm going to make this the coolest joint in the city, you just wait and watch.'

Haji Sahib appreciates his passion, loves the new menu card with the new biryani names, and tells him so, adding, 'Our customers seem to have taken to it too. You are talking about changing the look of the restaurant to match the changing times. I will talk to Hussain. No, I think it will be best if you talk to Hussain. If anyone can fight your case, it's him.' With that, Haji Sahib starts counting the number of biryani cauldrons—get set, go!

The cauldrons have sat in sections by name since the introduction of the new menu card. The young waiters bet on each ethnic prototype that walks in—which biryani will he order? A correct guess results in much backslapping and merriment. It's so entertaining that even Tayajee Tyyab sees the humour in it. Since the introduction of the new menu, Yahya has become a hot favourite with the cooks and the younger customers. And it is because of this knack for customer service and nose for business that Tayajee Tyyab wants him to start up immediately.

Bismillah Biryani happened some thirty years ago in the Burns Road kitchen of Ma Khatija. In the year 1952, all Memon Manzil's tykes were lost to be found in the kitchen of flat number 202, Tayajee Tyyab's boyhood home, where his mother was found cooking at all times.

Her delicious Memoni biryani became the talk of the neighbourhood, as did the history lesson she gave with it. Every fourteenth of the Muslim calendar month, Ma Khatija cooked biryani and shared it with the building's residents. She started the tradition in the wonder years of the fifties to help build treasured memories for the future, and the children who grew up around it were forever grateful for having experienced that time at Tayajee Tyyab's house.

During her childhood in Bombay, Khatija's great aunt Haleema Bai would often talk about family and friends gathering every other Friday at her Dada's house. 'Arey Khatija, those were delightful times, there was food, laughter, tears, bonding, friends, resolution of many a misunderstanding, seeds to create many conflicts, joy, sadness, clandestine meetings, love stories brewing, break-ups, but most of all togetherness.' Young Khatija had spent hours listening to stories about these 'Bombay gatherings' as she thought of them. To her, they were tales of intrigue, drama, sharing, caring and the coming together of relationships, and it was to breathe life into this past that she hosted the monthly 'Biryani aur kahani' at the

Burns Road flat. Tayajee Tyyab caught on to his mother's ideology of bringing people together over food and Bismillah Biryani came to be.

～

So here I am at Bismillah Biryani, whiling away my time sitting on the swivel chair facing the wall behind Tayajee Tyyab's desk that has a calligraphy-worked mirror hung on it, waiting for someone, anyone, to offer me a plate of biryani.

I spot Yahya in the calligraphy mirror as he walks in, heading for the stack of menus. He looks up as he hears the chair squeak, and then a little person stands up. That's me.

'Ya Bhai, how's it going?' I could not say Yahya when I was little, and settled on 'Ya'.

'Hey Ayesha, haven't seen you in a while, what's happening?'

'Nothing much, I'm trying to beat Snoopy in Snoopy Tennis at Nintendo, and to eat biryani since I got here, but no one seems to take the hint. Abbu glares at me and Tayajee is busy at the cash register. Can you help?' No point in not coming to the point.

'Of course, I practically own the place. Come on, let's get you the best plate on the house. Though I think you should leave the handheld Nintendo here, or give it to Hussain Uncle, otherwise you may lose it.'

'And everyone wonders why you are my favourite!' I look at him with adoring eyes, 'You get me Ya Bhai. It wasn't so hard for you to understand it's dinner time.'

'Let's go chow down some yummy biryani. I haven't had dinner as well,' says Yahya, grinning.

In my opinion, he has had a soft corner for me since I was born. He used to call me his 'little spitfire', since I was usually ready with a comeback. He's always been fun to talk to, and both of us aren't bothered that I am, well, let's say, a little chubby.

We leave the office and walk to the back of the restaurant where organized mayhem is in progress. The kitchen, a large room that looks like a biryani holding area, is frenetically busy. Men wearing red bandanas put biryani into packets, those with blue bandanas take them to the delivery window, and those with green bandanas take orders from the sea of humanity demanding to take home biryani. Haji Sahib sits at the cash register keeping a tight grip on the money transactions, right outside the red swinging door.

The kitchen door swings open and Ya Bhai and I spot Abbu and Tayajee Tyyab at the far left corner of the restaurant, sitting by the large poster that says Quetta. Abbu is stuffing tobacco into his pipe and Tayajee Tyyab is nodding a response to something that Abbu must have said. Ya Bhai turns to me, 'What Biryani do you want to eat today?'

'Sindhi biryani, with three drumsticks and three potatoes.'

'Well, little lady, Sindhi biryani has been renamed Ajrak Biryani. Here, look at the new menu,' he says, handing it to me.

'Wow, this is so cool Ya Bhai, so cool.'

'Cool, you think it's cool, now you see me making this joint really happening,' says Ya Bhai. My reaction to the menu seems to have reinforced his commitment, and it is in that moment, I think, that he realizes the stars *have* aligned in his favour.

'Ishaq, two plates triple drumstick Ajrak biryani and two cold drinks. Bring it to us in the office.'

∾

I am fascinated to learn that biryani has been around for hundreds of years. As Ya Bhai tells it, the story goes that Mumtaz Mahal, Shah Jahan's beloved empress, created the modern-day biryani.

My imagination takes me to the days of the Taj. I look down

at my now almost-devoured biryani serving and wonder about its perilous journey through time. Did it smell just like it does today, taste the same and cast the troops into a frenzy as it does the customers queued outside? Do all foods have a similar history, travelling with kings and conquerors, decorating the tables of queens and princesses, being enjoyed by peasants, troops and their rulers alike?

Was the East conquered for its spices? Was it really? Did travellers bring food and ingredients with them, and did the indigenous people adapt them to suit their palate and resources?

Yes, I nod my approval. Mumtaz Mahal deserves the Taj Mahal for gifting the subcontinent with the spicy biryani.

I lie in bed ready to fall asleep, with the history of biryani playing heavy on my mind. Unwittingly, my eyes focus on the play of light on the ceiling; the curtains are pulled back and passing cars cast flickering shadows on the walls. It is a fascinating light show, a lullaby of sorts, routine in comfort, reminiscent of childhood memories, sprinkled with wistful nostalgia and stardust of days to come.

～

Saturday mornings at Empress Market are one of my favourite things to do once a month. Ammi armed with a grocery list, Abbu with his enthusiasm, our driver Jahangir with non-stop chatter, and me just tagging along for the joy of it.

Empress Market is impressive rather than pretentious, unlike its namesake Queen Victoria. The bazaar is a rectangular single-storey building, with a large central atrium and four galleries surrounding it. The building is a Gothic structure with its frontage housing a tall central clock tower. The imperialists loved building clock towers. They may have gotten to countries on time but almost always overstayed their welcome, and while they stayed they enforced the locals to adopt some particularly British traits in lieu of national pride and homogenized spirit. Divide and conquer they did, and somehow made regional enthusiasm take precedence over national pride, which, according to my social studies teacher, was an unprofitable bargain for the indigenous population of the subcontinent.

Empress Market was completed in 1889, and named for Queen Victoria. The road adjacent to the colonial building is a disorderly spectacle of life and liberty that is colloquially Karachi. A disarray of buses, rickshaws, minibuses, wagons, motorbikes, scooters, cars, cycles and animal carts all going in the same general direction, without direction, and the chaos is speckled with foot traffic—men, women and children. A bus passes a few inches away from my car window, and within those inches I see a man squeezing his way through, as he walks between both vehicles. Oddly enough, he seems unperturbed by his proximity to the bus or car and that, in a nutshell, is Karachi.

People of all creeds and colours reside in this chaotic city—Parsee, Hindu, Christian, Makrani, Agha Khani, Bohri, Pathan, Punjabi, U.P.-wallay, Bengali, Delhi-wallay, Memon, Balouchi, Sindhi, Chinese, Kashmiri, Baltistani—and they move with the hurried pace of unruly traffic, living together in disorganized harmony, working, eating, praying, loving and breathing in this maximum city.

I step out of the car and follow my parents through the cacophony, the horns of the motors, the loud calls of the vendors, the traffic police screeching to control the uncontrollable, a throng of people everywhere. Absorbing Saturday morning sights, I walk purposefully towards the entrance, squeezing my girth to avoid bumping into people, but only momentarily. The savoury lemony smell of grilled corn on the cob, mixed with a whiff of vegetable fritters greets me as I walk to my favourite stop, Gul Khan Dry Fruits and Nuts. Luckily, it happens to be the third shop in the frontage gallery as we make a right through the clock tower entrance.

Getting to the shop is as enjoyable as lingering at its rim and stealing fistfuls from a mixed bag of nuts. The owner, Gul Khan, is very familiar with my antics and chatter, and unperturbed, he says, 'Stop stealing cashews, my child, sit on the rug inside and stick labels on the bags with Shabnum.'

My family haunts Gul Khan's Dry Fruit and Nuts, and this monthly routine of my parents shopping at the Empress Market, and me sitting doing hard labour and getting paid with sugar-coated nuts when leaving, charms me. I sit with Shabnum, Gul Lala's daughter, soaking in the incredible sensations, colours, sounds, smells, taste, touch. I pick up a handful of shelled pine nuts from a jute bag and roll them between my hands, the smooth tiny shell contains an incredibly delicious delight—chilgozay.

During winter holidays, I sit in the verandah with Dadi, drinking fresh orange juice and chowing on chilgozay for hours on end; we've had many a discussion on its buttery flavour and the joy it brings during the mild winters of Karachi.

The loud crash in the gallery draws my attention and I follow Gul Lala to Masala Centre next door. The smell of garam masala hits my sinuses as I notice the Pink Himalayan rock salt splattered on the large silver tray on the floor, and backtrack to avoid a full-on sinus attack.

The colours in Masala Centre make an impact like never before. I've been seeing spices all my life, the kitchen cabinet at home is well-stocked, but today I view them differently, Ya Bhai's voice ringing in my ears, 'Each spice has a name like you and me. Each one has a different flavour, like you and me. Each one has a purpose, like you and me. Each one is distinct, and passionately and lovingly changes the flavour of bland rice to the elegant pulao or the deliciously fiery biryani. Respect spices, it's the varying combination of these very spices that makes our cuisine distinctly Mughlai, desi, South Asian, subcontinental and Pakistani.'

Spices so vibrant with a taste so bold,
In centuries past they were priced as gold,
Lands were plundered for their worldwide spread,
Flavours of the Indus, became man's spicy dread.

◆

DUM BIRYANI

Ma Khatija sat with the building's children in flat 202 and told them biryani tales, 'Empress Mumtaz Mahal is credited for the modern-day biryani; she felt it was a complete meal and suggested the troops be fed with it during both wartime and peace.'

Looking at the rapt young faces, she continued, 'The evolution of biryani from pulao is fascinating. History suggests that the "dum" method of cooking comes from the Arab or Persian style of cooking, and may have travelled to the Indian subcontinent from Persia. The meat is placed separately in a marinade of curd, spices and papaya and cooked till tender. Then it is layered with parboiled rice, infused with droplets of rose water, saffron and mace. These spices give it a flowery and royal essence.'

'Then it is sealed in a handi and set on a low flame until the rice is fully cooked, plumped and ready to serve. Did you know that biryani is different across different regions of the subcontinent?' And then she continued, 'They all claim their biryani is the best. Despite all the different versions—Sindhi biryani with potatoes, Memoni biryani with spicy masala, kacha gosht biryani cooked in whole garam masala *sans* tomatoes—it is actually Lucknow that lays the ultimate claim. Called Awadhi dum biryani, its speciality is that the meat is first half cooked, and then the dish is brought to perfection through the dum pukth style of cooking, almost like the ancient times when berian was buried into the ground until the rice plumped.'

Ingredients

3 to 4 lb mutton (leg meat)
3 mugs basmati rice
6 to 10 oz oil
2½ to 3 large onions, sliced
4 tsp freshly chopped garlic and garlic
Salt to taste
Red chilli powder to taste
Whole garam masala (10 green cardamom pods, ½ to ¾ tsp peppercorns, ½ to ¾ tsp cloves, 2 to 4 cinnamon sticks, 5 black cardamom pods)
16 to 20 oz yogurt
6 to 8 green chillies
½ bunch coriander leaves
Orange food colour (a pinch)
8 to 16 oz water
Dash of lemon juice
2 tbsp kewra water

Ingredients to be added to boiling rice

Salt to taste
4 bay leaves
Whole garam masala (4 cinnamon sticks, 3 black cardamom pods, ¼ tsp black peppercorns, ¼ tsp cloves)

Method
Masala

Heat oil and fry half the amount of sliced onions till brown. Remove and set aside.

Heat oil and add meat, the remaining sliced onions, ginger, garlic, salt, red chilli powder and whole garam masala. Cook until half done, adding brown onions (fried earlier) yogurt and lemon juice. Once the meat is tender, set it aside. The biryani masala is ready.

Rice

In a separate pot, boil water for rice adding whole garam masala, and bay leaves. Once water comes to a boil add pre-soaked rice and cook till tender crisp. Drain rice, and layer half of it in a separate pot, topping with a layer of biryani masala. Add the second layer of rice and top with fried onions. Sprinkle food colouring, cilantro, mint, pinch of garam masala powder and 2 tbsp kewra water. Seal pot with foil and lid. Cook on full heat for 5 minutes and medium to low heat for 15 minutes to complete the dum. Let it sit for 10 minutes, mix and serve.

Garnish with green chillies, mint and chopped cilantro. Serve with a side of kachumber salad (chopped onions, tomatoes and green chillies) and raita.

◆

HARYALEE BIRYANI

Biryani, to love or to love a little more, that is the question. If you are from the subcontinent then you may have asked yourself this question when faced with a biryani platter. Why do we love it so much? Is it the aroma, the flavour, the presentation, or that it is a complete food in itself and hits all senses at once, invoking the passions of the foodies and not-so-foodies?

Ingredients
1 bunch coriander
1 bunch mint
10 serrano peppers
15 blanched almonds
2½ tbsp coconut powder
1 tbsp ginger and garlic, finely chopped
1 cup yogurt
1¼ chicken (approximately 19 to 20 pieces)
3 medium-sized red onions
⅓ cup to ½ cup oil
Salt to taste
½ cup water
3 red potatoes
1 bay leaf
1 tbsp kewra water
½ tsp garam masala powder
3 mugs rice

Ingredients to be added to boiling water
Whole garam masala (10 to 15 black peppercorns, 5 to 10 cloves, 5 green cardamom pods, 1 black cardamom pod, 1 cinnamon stick, 2 bay leaves, 1 tsp salt)

Method
Slice onions thinly and fry in hot oil until golden brown, set aside half the fried onions. Add finely chopped ginger-garlic and chicken to the onions remaining in the pan. Cook on high heat for a few minutes.

In a blender, blend coriander, mint, green serrano peppers, ½ cup water, blanched almonds and coconut powder. Once blended, add this green mixture, yogurt and salt to the chicken (note: the green colour will lighten with addition of yogurt). Now add peeled and halved potatoes, cooking on high to medium heat, add a little water if green masala looks too dry. Cook until oil separates and the chicken and potatoes are tender.

In a separate pot boil 8 to 10 mugs of water and add the bay leaf, 1 tsp salt and whole garam masala. Bring to boil. Add pre-soaked rice to boiling water, boiling it till tender-crisp. Drain rice.

Now layer a pot with half the rice. Add chicken and potatoes cooked in the green masala on top of the rice. Add second layer of rice, sprinkle garam masala powder, fried onions, kewra water, seal pot with foil and lid. Cook on full heat for 5 minutes, and medium to low heat for 15 minutes to complete the dum. Let it sit for 10 minutes and serve.

Chapter 2

Sindh

Palla or Hilsa, What's in a Name?

I turn my face and stare at the sea. The tide is low, it is the end of November and the sea is pushed way back, the waves roll at a distance. The skies are blue, as is the sea and my spirit. The sun hides behind a stubborn cloud and I yell 'Move cloud,' and to my chagrin, the sun intervenes and says, no need to look out for me child, I look after myself, much like you. No one can stop me from shining, no one can stop my light.

I am not like you sun, well, maybe, since I'm round, but that's where the similarity ends. And the cloud moves, and the sun shines, and the wind whispers to me, 'Let me explain, you are not like the sun, you are better than the sun.'

What? How can I be better than the sun? The wind blows me a kiss, and stops as suddenly as it began.

The gentle roar of the sea surges forward as if saying, take a deep breath and let yourself go, much like the little branch that trusts the running river to take it to its destination. Be the branch and let your mother be the running river, the rushing stream, the flowing water; she will never disenchant you.

It is a soulful evening and there is serenity to the sea, in much contradiction to my soul. There are no crashing waves, just a lull to the water, much like the bored dog that sits on the shore looking at it. The lone camel rider beckons me to ride the sands of the shore. Maybe he thinks I'm a visitor to the city. No sir, I am a Karachiite. And the young couple walking hand in hand starts running, swishing sand under their feet. A seagull makes a graceful landing on the placid water, much like a ballerina performing to Tchaikovsky's 'Swan Lake'.

I turn my head sighting the pink casino building, faded, jaded and waiting to be put to some good use. Bhutto built it but someone killed it, that's all I know.

At a distance I see the island of Manora; what fun it must be to live on it. A passing car honks and I unwittingly turn to the sound of the horn, and my gaze focuses on the apartment complex hoarding the seashore. The flats could do with a coat of fresh paint. The real-estate builder must hire a professional to beautify the façade of the apartment complex.

I step onto the sand and start building a castle, escaping from my recent conversation with Ammi, and try to distance myself from the exchange. I wish to erase it from my mind but I can't. She says it gently, simply and eloquently, and then walks away as if to give me a little time to let her words sink in. I watch her walk away, her head tilted to the side as she looks to the sea, lost in thought, thinking about me, or perhaps her mother. If she had lost her temper, the way she usually does when referring to my excess weight, I would not have felt this guilty or obligated to do the needful.

Suddenly it starts to rain, the horizon becomes a mist and the walkers start to run, but I keep sitting on the wet sand. The rain pours faster, and I start crying. The rain pours hard, as do my tears. I cry for my mother, I cry because her mother died before I was born, I cry because she was never loved by another who is a mother, I cry because I never knew my Nani, I cry because I never chose to look like my Nani but I do, I cry because my mother longs to see her mother in me as I grow, I cry because I want my mother to be able to see her mother's face in mine, and lastly I cry because to accomplish that I have to lose fifty pounds.

The rain stops suddenly, gone is the passing cloud, the city looks washed, the apartment complex looks as if freshly painted and the grass looks green on all sides. I run to my mother, embrace her, and we start our journey to a place called home.

～

The lunch bell rings, I grab my lunch box and walk out of class. Lost in thought, I waddle to the picnic benches near the swings at the back of the school. Sofia, my best friend, will meet me soon, I bring homemade lunch while she always buys her lunch at the school canteen and joins me a few minutes into the lunch break. I look up and see our new principal looking intently at me, her gaze transfixed. I look to my left and right, unsure why the principal is staring at me. Am I in trouble?

'I've seen you before, much earlier, who are you?'

I nervously play with the handle of my lunch box, accidentally unclipping the lid and spilling the contents, releasing the effervescence of freshly made pulao.

'Shireen, pulao, Shireen,' Mother Geraldine whispers, wide-eyed, as if looking at a ghost.

'No, I'm Ayesha. Shireen was my Nani, and she died a long time ago.'

～

'Dadi, Hilsa is much superior in taste to Palla,' Jalal declares with utmost authority and slight condemnation. 'We Bengalis know our fish. Palla is just the poor cousin on the other side of the river.'

'Nonsense, Hilsa and Palla are the same fish. It's just that the Sindhis make it better than you do,' retorts Dadi with tongue-in-cheek, to which Jalal storms off pretending offense, but not before sticking his tongue out at her.

'What's with the Hilsa-Palla controversy?' I ask, while playing with a broken end of a knot that's come undone in the cane sofa. 'And this sofa is already coming apart, no wonder the Mughals lost the empire and the land. They can't even weave a durable sofa.'

Sofia, defender of the underdog, will have none of that. 'Rather harsh, not to say condescending, Ayesha,' she snaps, rocking the chair that is usually my seat on the verandah. 'It's seen three years of wear and tear and so the cane's coming undone. You can't blame the cane furniture-maker for his ancestor being deposed from the throne.'

My best friend, sixteen-year-old Sofia champions the poor, generously shares her personal savings with paupers on the street, distributes her pocket money amongst the domestic staff—nanny, maid, cook, waiter, guard, driver—and never fails to reprimand my adolescent arrogance. Compassionate Sofia is a hippy spirit, she falls in love frequently, charms many a young man with her natural coyness, shares her riches with joy, and eats the entire kitchen without gaining an ounce. She is a pretty girl, with an almost Demi Moore kind of attraction, dark hair and dark eyes set in a small angular face with a cute button nose and full lips. Boys find her attractive, and Ya Bhai is on the top of that list.

'I don't blame Bahadur Shah Zafar, he was just weak and crumbled to the cunning of the British Empire. It's Aurangzeb I loathe, his orthodox brand of Islam, hunger and greed for the throne, a complete dichotomy in my eyes, led to the destruction and Anglicization of the rich subcontinent. If only secular Dara Shikoh had ruled maybe the cane furniture walla would have been educated, and his sons and daughters would have inherited more than just skill to weave cane. Makes one wonder, Prince Charles is leading the good life, while the heir to the Mughal throne weaves cane furniture to make ends meet. It's tragic,' I retort, 'and abhorrent!'

'Well, you have a strange way of showing your contempt for the British Raj and the House of Windsor. It sounds more like disdain for the Mughals,' declares Sofia.

'I love the Mughals and I'd marry a Mughal prince in a heartbeat,' I offer as my parting shot, on my way out the door to Hyderabad.

I have been starving myself for a week, almost. Living on apples, tea and boiled eggs, simply to chow down earthen bowls filled with rabri, drink gallons of thadal and devour thick slices of the Bombay Bakery coffee cake on my day-trip to Hyderabad.

❧

Hyderabad

The buzz in Hyderabad's Shahi Bazaar is electric; noise, people, food stalls, the 'chhun chhun' of the Hyderabadi Sindhi bangles, music, and the loud evening Asr *azaan* playing lyrics to the carnival of life. I walk a hurried pace to Rabri and Kheer Centre, hoping to beat the pedestrian traffic customarily headed the same way after Asr prayers. Amidst the madness of the rush hour I spot the dessert shop diagonal to Navalrai Clock Tower, the colonial landmark I am so desperately looking for.

I block the din and focus on my bowl of rabri, my anticipatory gnawing insides ready to savour the sweetness of the delicious dessert, eager to taste the layers of thickened milk skin reduced to condensed perfection. I am euphoric, losing seven pounds in one week was worth it, and I am determined to gain it back through an indulgent feast of rabri and Bombay Bakery coffee cake.

I muse the journey of the milk; the fodder consumed by the cow so its body can produce milk, and the calf denied its feed so it may instead be transported to Rabri and Kheer Centre where begins the slow cooking of the milk to reduce its water content—in essence encouraging its creaminess and natural sweetness centre stage—the low heat gradually evaporating the water, until only cream and sugar and the heady scent of cardamom remain. I sit in a state of sweet nirvana focusing on the simplicity and joy of the moment—milk and sugar served in an earthen bowl.

Yes, simple pleasures make the best treasures.

～

Makli Hill, Thatta

It is so quiet, the sound of silence is deafening.

I am not a fan of silence, only rarely, but since I stepped onto the ancient Makli grounds there has been nothing but quiet, intense quiet. My gaze falls onto the landscape ahead, a wide open terracotta space with thousands of marked and unmarked gravestones; these buried bones were alive once, like me they must have been born to a mother and a father, been mothers and fathers themselves, maybe dreamers, kings, paupers, criminals, lovers, belonging to different religions but all buried in the same graveyard, same dirt.

Despite Dadi's teachings, I believe that death takes all to the same place, our recycled body becomes dust to dust, ashes to ashes, recycled, poof, gone, and our spirit answers to one God.

God of all things considered.

The morning drive into lower Sindh was enthralling. The highway meandered through sporadic greenery, a few dry patches and fields of yellow flowers. For a moment, I thought, I was in Central Punjab, but no, this is my Sindh, my home, my land, the province of the Indus and the Arabian Sea.

Rural life sat idle and waved enthusiastically, and each time our minibus passed a group of children, the driver honked a funny tune and slowed down a bit. The children laughed in joy, waved ecstatically, and sometimes did a jubilant dance on the side of the road. The bus finally stopped at Makli and now I stand here absorbing the magnificence of the expansive fourteenth-century burial site, home to more than half-a-million graves, a sight of Spartan beauty and much historical significance.

The massive cemetery is dotted with shrines, tombs and the scenic path is a treasure trove of ancient historic handiwork; circular designs and motifs, openings and intricately designed arches, majestic rotundas, blue tile and terracotta carvings: extensive Islamic calligraphic art juxtaposed with lavish Hindu traditions of Rajasthani art adorning the tombs of the dead.

I gaze and immerse myself in the history of the ancient burial site. Zahid, our guide and owner of the Indus Guiding Club gives us a perspective on the variety of stonework and carvings, 'It is a perfect union of Persian and Arab influence and the traditions of the Indus-Aryan Sanatana Dharma. The confluence of the two is depicted in much of the craftwork here.

'There are three major periods dividing the style of work,' he says, 'The first one being the Summa dominance of the region, ranging from the fourteenth to the sixteenth century; the Tarkhan and Arghun periods during much of the sixteenth century; and the Mughal dynasty up until the end of the eighteenth century.'

He points ahead, 'Look at that impressive square sandstone

structure marking the tomb of Jam Nizamuddin. The stone is dressed with floral and decorative patterns, a popular element in carvings from the Samma period. It is brilliant, majestic and awe-inspiring, and should have been as well-known if not more than the Roman Forum and Palatine Hill in Rome, and would have been but for the ignorance of the people of Pakistan. We failed to market this as an international tourist attraction. This, coupled with the ruins of Mohenjo-daro, Taxila and the Gandhara civilization—the region sits on a goldmine of history.'

I shake my head in disappointment (as I invariably do), at the pathetic what is, what was, and what could have been.

I wonder if Italian and Egyptian primary school students learn about the ancient civilizations of the Indus—Gandhara and Harappa—or whether, much like us, they only focus on the glorious past of Pompeii and the Pyramids.

Do they savour pulao, cake rusk, and pakoray, the way we devour pizza, falafel and pasta?

I look at a young Khawajasira, a cross-dresser of sorts. He suddenly catches my eye, claps his hands, and declares in a high-pitched voice, 'Baji, hire me to tell you stories of the graveyard. Here, the dead walk amongst the living, not like in the city, where people walk with a dead conscience and breathe like the living. Arey hire me Baji, I will only charge you hundred rupees for a two-hour history lesson.'

I laugh out loud, hand him pocket-change telling him a history lesson is not a prerequisite. He tucks the red notes into his stuffed bra, curls his scarlet lipstick-laden thick lips into a wide smile, claps his hands hard, winks at me mischievously and declares, 'You have been beautiful for centuries, and he's dashing too.'

'Who?' I ask curious.

He winks again, smiles knowingly, runs down Makli Hill and

slowly vanishes into the horizon.

'Ayesha, Ayesha, Ayesha, chalo, we are headed to Keenjhar lake, let's get a move on!' Sofia's loud command might wake up the dead, and I find myself rushing to my group.

Zahid, our group leader, does a quick headcount as we head on our way to the city of Thatta and later, Keenjhar lake for tea; great photography and much awaited chit-chat by the lake. 'Hey Soofs, have you ever asked your parents why they spelt your name SOFIA on the birth certificate instead of SOPHIA?' I ask, wondering why it never struck me to ask her this earlier.

Sofia bends and picks up a tiny rock as we saunter to the bus parked on the side of the dirt road by a very marked entrance that reads 'Makli Cemetery, UNESCO, A World Heritage Site'. 'Mummy says SOPHIA is too Americanized, and since the Greek, Italian, Latin, or better still the ancient spelling of the name is SOFIA, she decided to stick to the archaic spelling, much like this graveyard.'

'That sounds so damn morbid, comparing it to Makli,' I say. 'This Walkman is a great invention, I wish I had rechargeable batteries though, most of my pocket money goes into buying these A-4 batteries to keep music alive. My walks around the Auntie Park are sane and surviving because of this very man I walk with, Mr Walkman.'

'Twenty-one and without a real man, yup, Mr Walkman is the only man you are walking with in the foreseeable future,' quips Sofia as she trips on an Apple Sidra bottle, catches herself and continues, 'Yaar you know the drink Thadal, the traditional Sindhi sherbet, so refreshing, I'm hoping to get an authentic flavour of the drink on our Mehraan jaunt today.'

～

Why I felt a compelling need to visit the Shah Jahan Mosque in Thatta, I don't know, but I'm here now and the mosque beckons me. I take off my slippers and walk through the red arches of the mosque. The blue Hala tile work is exquisite, intricate calligraphic writings and a sudden cool breeze whispering a call to prayer; with it many walking into the mosque, and the beginning of 'Allah Hu Akbar, Allah Hu Akbar,' the tremendous echo of the afternoon Zuhr azaan is loud and serene all at once, bringing to mind the mention of acoustics when I researched the mosque. The acoustics of Shah Jahan Mosque are famed to be such that the call to prayer is heard throughout the mosque, and city, without electric amplification, hence the city-dwellers of the seventeenth century must have heard the very sound I hear today.

This magnificent mosque was built as a tribute to the people of Thatta. When Jahangir, or maybe it was his vicious wife Nur Jahan, exiled Shah Jahan from Delhi in the earlier part of the seventeenth century, it is said that Shah Jahan sought refuge in Thatta for some time. On his succession to the throne, Emperor Shah Jahan built this mosque to thank the locals for their hospitality. If only the Mughals were thankful to each other as a family, the carnage and blood-fest that manifested due to lack of primogeniture would have been avoided.

Pathetic, tragic, a lesson in time, or maybe plain old karma of sins of the fathers and forefathers, and now I stand at the main entrance of the mosque and ponder the grandeur and splendour of the site, an intricate welcome fountain, once lush gardens, brilliant blue tile mixed with red brick, countless domes, plentiful arches and a glorious past. And once again my mind takes me to the furniture maker. What must he feel each time he visits a Mughal site? Grateful for not living his life under the Damocles sword, or regretful that his ancestors lost the Kohinoor Diamond and Peacock

Throne to pirates from faraway lands, I wonder.

Damn this game of thrones, commoners at least died a natural death.

∼

A visit to an authentic home of a local Sindhi family and their warm welcome to the tour-guide's guests, was the lunch arrangement that Indus Guiding Club promised those who booked a trip with them into the lower Sindh belt. And to experience this small-city welcome one must drive to the real Sindh, considered sans Karachi, according to the conventional wisdom of the middle class in Pakistan.

We entered the house and I observed the room rather sceptically, but the geniality of the young lad named Janoo, and the room itself was welcoming. The small square room served as a sitting room, dining room and drawing room, and sometimes a guestroom with the arrival of the not-so-occasional overnight guest, the norm eastern culture is webbed around. Relatives, friends and accompanying strangers are always welcome to spend the night, share a meal and form a bond.

The absence of a sofa made the room appear larger than it was. In one corner were two hand-painted chairs sitting low and woven with jute rope, and a small end-table nestled between the chairs, the red and blue hues of the handcrafted furniture brought cheer to the room; well-suited to host a homemade meal and chit-chat to follow. A thick caramel-coloured carpet covered the floor, and coupled with the cool air emanating from the room air cooler the setting promised a dreamless reverie on a warm spring afternoon.

The walls of the room were painted a clean crisp white, and two of the four walls were adorned with pictures, paintings and handicrafts telling tales of the land. I found myself drawn to a picture of the Thar Desert, endless sand dunes, blazing sun, a gazelle, a child and endless possibilities. I touched the photo, momentarily overwhelmed by the harsh yet tender exactness of nature captured in that one timeless shot.

Zahid, our guide, spoke up, 'I took that photo and made the frame too. It was my present to Janoo's family on my last trip to Thar a few weeks ago.' Before I could respond to him, Fahmeeda Soomro, Janoo's mother and the mistress of the house, walked in with German silver glasses of homemade Thadal.

Sofia and I thanked her, and I could see that Zahid's artistic sensitivity had momentarily caught Sofia's attention. My best friend's latest love story was about to begin. We sat down at the *ralli dasterkhwan* and started chatting with the other ten in the group. There was a German lady with her Pakistani husband and fourteen-year-old twin boys; an older couple with their almost seventeen-year-old granddaughter and her friend; Ajit Samra, a photographer from a local magazine; and Ameena Abbasi, a school teacher teaching English Literature, History and Classics in Translation at Convent of Jesus and Mary in Karachi.

Fahmeeda was an instant hit with the group. She offered everyone Thadal and announced, 'Fry Palla fish is fresh from the river and right on your plate.'

'Could I have mine steamed?' I asked as politely as I could, sipping Thadal. Steamed, boiled, broiled, oil-free, strained, baked, and any other cooking technique—I had unwittingly become very familiar with all of them. My weight-loss journey had been tremendously educative. Genius being one per cent inspiration and ninety-nine per cent perspiration, Nani's unrealized legacy and my perspiration did a victory dance at the finish line.

It took me fifty-eight long months to reach my goal of losing fifty pounds, but I did. The day the weighing scale stopped at ninety-five, I did too. I had crumbled to the bathroom floor, bare, weightless, and shed tears to match the August monsoon outside the window. I was elated, aware of the bounties waiting my new arrival into a magnificent and chaotic world, ready, thanks to my one per cent inspiration, to live inside the reality that was once a dream.

The impact of childhood obesity was more than skin deep. It was an almost intellectual and deliberate effort on my part to understand my love story with food. The pleasure derived from tasting, savouring, soaking in the sensations associated with pleasure eating, the shame in overeating, and the eventual menacing weight gain that comes with solitary eating—why? Much like an addict and an alcoholic I satisfied my addiction in solitary confinement away from the judging and probing eyes of the world.

What led me to overeat?

What made me eat more and more, and not stop until I finally did?

What changed in my relationship with food that allowed me to drop the excess baggage of overweight?

What changed in my relationship with myself, my family and society that made me want to find myself under layers of flesh?

Was my weight loss an imperfect means to a perfect end, or was it the other way around?

Was denial of one of the greatest pleasures in life, yo-yo and fad dieting the only solutions towards attaining a beautiful body?

So many questions but not enough answers, some answers were simple, some not so much.

～

Dadi and Ya Bhai are giving me a lecture on adopting an improved eating regimen. Whenever they get together, bashing my eating habits becomes their favourite pastime.

What do they know about my struggles?

What do they know about protein and carbohydrates, and how mixing them up is not ideal?

Seriously, someone stop them, now, and with that thought in my head I yell, 'Ammi, Mom, Mother, come here, now. Put a stopper on Ya Bhai, and tell Dadi to quit lecturing me.'

'You are telling me that the pairing of roti and meat curry, egg and paratha, mutton biryani, puri and choley, nihari and naan, is wrong? People have been pairing these foods for centuries. Centuries!' responds an exasperated Ya Bhai.

'Well, Ya Bhai, I think you just want your B. Bees to keep selling biryani—carbohydrates and protein together on a plate. You're not going to convince me. And I'm not saying that I am cutting carbs from my diet, but this protein thing is a new fad diet that I may want to try out. Yup, that's it.'

'Ayesha, carbohydrates and proteins are building blocks, and our ancestors were pairing them together for a reason. Nature has blessed us with so many different kinds of foods for a reason, foods complement each other and are meant to be eaten together,' interjects Dadi to settle the almost brawl between me and Ya Bhai. What do these two know about losing weight? A seventy-five-year-old grandma and a twenty-eight-year-old nouveau business owner, zero, nada, zilch!

Nadir, my older brother, is sprawled on the newest addition to the verandah furnishings, a green leather beanbag, and from the look in his eye he's excited to see a street fight break out between yours truly and Ya Bhai.

'Yahya, you are right man, Ayesha is a nut! I still haven't figured out what kind of nut, but a nut for sure.'

I glare at Nadir. I'll kill him one of these days.

'She's not a nut, she's a raisin, shrivelled, small, brown and adored by the old people of the world,' Sameer my younger brother says on cue. I'm going to kill him too.

Time to plug the ears and close the eyes and put on the headphones and listen to 'I Go to Extremes', by Billy Joel. I drift off, thinking of all the random stuff that's been important in my life of late.

Walkman: Thank God for the Walkman, my escape from Dadi's lectures on healthy eating and ragging by the boys.

Angst: Every time people discuss my weight and choose to give me advice in a sagely Nestor-esque tone I want to scream. I think I know a little more about weight loss than them.

Protein: Chicken, eggs, mutton, fish and some other foods that cannot be mixed with a side of carbs, at least for now.

Beef: I don't eat it, it bloats me.

Carbs: I love carbs, I could live on carbs; roti, rice, papay (tea rusk), biscuits, pound cake, cake rusk.

Apples, Eggs and Tea: I once lived on apples, boiled eggs and tea for ten days—lost seven pounds, and a little bit of my mind as well.

Biryani and Biscuit: If I get marooned on an island, it has to be with biryani and biscuits.

Music: I love music—English, Urdu, Hindi, Punjabi, Sufi Music—it's all music to my ears.

Lasix: A pill my father takes, occasionally, to reduce water retention and help stabilize his high blood pressure. I sometimes jip it from his medicine pouch to get rid of my bloating. A girl's got to look good in the morning, after an indulgent night of high sodium intake from chilli chips and diet coke. Of late I've been using it often;

I've been picking up a pack from the pharmacy for personal use.

Auntie Park: I love walking it off, weight, angst, frustration. Auntie Park is behind the British Embassy and a ten-minute drive from the house. I'm found there weekdays in the evening, come hail, storm, strike or tension in the city except public holidays, of course.

Best friend: Met her a lifetime ago.

❧

Salma Khala is Ammi's older sister. She makes the best karhi this side of the Wagah, lives in Karachi and has no daughters—therefore, expectedly her love affair with me is intense—and her love affair with the conviction of marrying me to one of her sons, still more intense. Obviously that is not on my agenda, but it is on Salma Khala's, so today she has sent me her mouth-watering pakora-laden homemade karhi to rein me in. Mind you, I adore my Khala, but I adore myself more, and as I taste the karhi I think of Fahmeeda Soomro's story of Noori feeding Jam Tamachi, karhi on their wedding night. How authentic the story is, your guess is as good as mine, but surely karhi, as delicious as it may be, must not be consumed right after the nikaah ceremony—that was my take-home lesson from the story.

Jam Tamachi died roaming the Thar Desert and is buried at Makli, and Noori is buried on a small island in Keenjhar lake. According to an urban legend, her spirit remains desperate to reach land and search for Jam Tamachi.

Salma Khala is a replica of my great grandfather, and a handsome woman she is. It's fascinating how the same faces keep coming back—I look like my Nani, Salma Khala looks like her Dada, and Farhad Mamu, my mother's brother, well, I'm sure, he looks like someone too. I wonder if it's coincidence or destiny that takes us down the road of bearing the burdens of our forefathers— either way, it is a heavy load to carry. We carry the burden of our ancestors through genetics, relationships, choices and unfinished business, and time, society and food become the vessel that moves us forward to complete these abandoned or unfinished endeavours.

The doctrine of karma and samsara in Indian philosophy brings a harmony to our universe; they play the great equalizer maintaining a steady balance; an equilibrium of cause and effect. Though sometimes the cause generates collateral damage where the affected may be someone else, other than the one initiating the cause. Consequently, sometimes the sins of the father come back to roost at a time when the son may not be willing, or able to pay with blood. Consequently, Samsara is my favourite perfume to wear currently. I wonder what binds my spirit to the material world.

Maybe one day I'll have my answer.

He brings us back with the same faces,
Different fates, with ancient traces,
Our faiths may be different, we nourish the same,
It's a marvellous story, not a game.

KARHI

We all have our own unique love affair with karhi. Ammi, Dadi, Nani, Khala, or Phuppo, at least one of the five makes the best karhi in a desi family, either side of the Wagah. Yes, we South Asians have a lot more in common than we like to focus on. Our love for family, extended family, food, cricket and our commonality of culture, language and skin colour make us one people. We are the sub-continentals of this wonderful world.

In our family Salma Khala makes the best karhi, and a family get-together over karhi–chawal, shami kabab, kachumbar salad (finely chopped onion, tomato, green chilli and cilantro seasoned with white vinegar and lemon juice), achar and chutney is always a delight to savour.

How is one to describe karhi? It is a besan and yogurt-based sauce with fritters or pakoray. The Rajasthanis or Marwaris, Gujaratis, Sindhis and Punjabis all have their unique styles of making karhi. All ethnicities differ a little in flavour and texture but for the most part the basic ingredients of the dish remain the same, pakora or sans pakora at times. Though it is to be mentioned that karhi is originally a Rajasthani dish, and its derivations by other ethnicities are happenstance of proximity and travel.

The cuisine of Rajasthan is greatly influenced by the scarcity of water and its arid lands. The region is drought-ridden but its wonderfully rich heritage and vibrant people have learnt to adapt and have evolved a cuisine that contributes immensely to the food delights of the subcontinent. Since water is scarce, food is mostly milk-, yogurt- or ghee-based, lending it a unique texture, depth and richness, typical of Rajasthani cuisine. Water and fresh greens are substituted with dairy, hence the use of water is minimized in the cooking of food.

Rajasthani–Marwari cuisine is mostly vegetarian (sans fresh greens) and encompasses a beautifully colourful and rich variety of specialties. It is robust like its history, region and inhabitants. The desert gypsies of yesteryears helped in the evolution of this desert cuisine. Food that lasted for several days and could be eaten without heating, was preferred.

Lentils, besan and beans obtained from native plants are used extensively for cooking in the desert belts of Rajasthan, hence karhi is an obvious outcome. The neighbouring states of Punjab, Gujarat and Haryana borrowed the besan-based karhi pakora from Rajasthan and gave it a flavour of their own.

Punjabi karhi is thicker (sans jaggery), and potatoes and spinach are commonly dipped in the pakora batter, as are onions in the yogurt base; while Gujarati karhi is usually sans pakoray. Needless to say, the variations are delicious and are commonly enjoyed with boiled rice.

When it was time for me to make the original curry, I used Salma Khala's recipe, a family recipe dating back to the mid-nineteenth century.

Ingredients

For the yogurt base

1 kg yogurt (beat with water, 2 to 3 glasses to make the consistency thin)
1 cup besan (mix with 1 to 2 cups water and beat well ensuring a smooth thin consistency, add to yogurt through sieve, and mix well)
2 medium onions, diced
1 tsp ginger
1 tsp garlic
1½ tsp turmeric
Salt to taste
1 tsp red chilli powder

Ingredients for pakoray

1 cup besan
1 green chilli, chopped
4 tbsp chopped spinach
1 medium-sized potato, finely diced
3 tbsp chopped cilantro
Salt to taste
Red chilli powder to taste
½ tsp ajwain, ½ tsp coriander seeds, 1 tsp cumin seeds (pan roasted and roughly ground)
½ to 1 tsp baking powder (level)

Ingredients for fried garnish (bhagar)
Oil
1½ onions, sliced
Dried red chilli whole (4 to 6)
Curry leaves (optional)

Method
Mix ingredients for karhi as mentioned above and bring to a boil, stirring all along. Cook for 3 to 3½ hours on medium heat, adding water as and when the mixture starts to thicken, maintaining a thin consistency. Keep stirring periodically to ensure the consistency and ensure that no dough balls form.

Towards the end of the cooking period, mix ingredients for the pakoray as mentioned above to form fairly thick non-runny batter. Fry the pakoray and add them to the karhi. Mix and turn off heat. Prepare fried garnish (bhagar), pour it on to the karhi and serve with a side of boiled rice.

◆

FRIED PALLA FISH

Ingredients
1 Palla fish
Oil for frying

Ingredients for Masala (grind in coffee grinder)
Salt
½ tsp Red chilli powder
¾ tsp Coriander powder
10 to 15 Pomegranate seeds

Method

Rub salt on fish and set aside. Wash Palla thoroughly, shallow fry until done (it's very quick). Sprinkle masala instantly after taking off fire and pour hot oil on top; the oil that was used to fry the fish in.

❧

Chapter 3

Treasures of Makran

Sajji, from Balochistan to Bulandshar to Karachi

1995

Faiz kept hitting the ball with the racquet, the harder he hit the better he felt, *keep hitting, keep hitting, keep hitting, either until the racquet breaks, the squash ball cracks or the wall crumbles.* None of the three happened and he finally gave up. Exhausted, panting and thirsty he sat on the floor of the squash court drained physically but charged emotionally.

He thought about getting a club sandwich from Spinzer, but on second thoughts decided against it since it wasn't the best thing to eat when preparing for a squash tournament in a week, and instead headed to his car parked inside the gates of the club and made his way home. As he pulled into the porch he saw a house full of family, sitting in the lawn enjoying the balmy Karachi evening.

The large lawn lay to the right of the porch, long and rectangular, thickly bordered by red, yellow, white, orange and pink rose bushes, set against a lush green backdrop of grass. The fragrance of their flowering blooms danced in the air. Countless potted money plants, a large mango tree, fiery trees of flame of the forest, shrubs and creepers dotted the garden, making it inviting.

Faiz's mother, like all mothers from Pakistan, pampered her garden as she did her children and it had blossomed into a sitting area that resounded with talk and laughter. Every evening the cook unfolded chairs under the shade of the large mango tree and one by one the family, extended family, and sometimes neighbours too, made their way to her garden where she sat waiting with a tea trolley, ready to pour and serve a hot cup of chai with a side of sizzling gossip or gup shup.

Faiz walked into a full-house session. The laughter was loud, the tea hot, and the trolley laden with desi homemade goodies. Faiz's older sister Mehreen sat pretty alongside the parents. He found a spot on the grass next to his twin brother Zaid.

The young men were identical twins but with very different dispositions. Zaid was a man of numbers with a businessman's personality—practical, methodical, organized, punctual and focused on ambitious aspirations, with a steady march towards achieving them. He was the son who had left the soil, made his home elsewhere with a career in finance and banking.

Faiz on the flip side was an artist by nature, an uneasy spirit, driven to the sciences for the practical aspect of pursuing a career coupled with a passion to improve upon the infrastructure in Pakistan. Alas, being a dreamer was not a practical pursuit, and in the real world to only remain an idealist's dream. Mehreen broke into his thoughts, 'How was squash and how many racquets did you break today?' she quipped.

'How many do you think?' he retorted.

Mehreen's character was straight out of an A.R. Khatoon novel, a cultured U.P.-wallee to the core, much like her mother, but with an extra dose of gossip, curiosity, manipulation and drama. Her penchant for family intrigue and exaggerated truths had gained her quite a reputation on either side of the family and amongst her in-laws. With eyes and ears wide open she was the person to contact for all ensuing amongst family and friends. 'Hey, I think I found just the right girl to introduce you to,' she said, looking at the twins, handing Faiz a cup of chai and a samosa.

'Too, to, or two?' asked Faiz laughing, 'And how do you know which one of us would be better suited to meet her?'

'I'll introduce you both, and then maybe you can fight a duel, or better still fight it out on the squash court. Whoever wins, gets the girl,' she replied with a glint in her eye.

Faiz gave her ready response, a thumbs up, and said, 'You can introduce her to Zaid.' And winking at his brother he took his leave and headed into the house to change. His Dada was sitting in the foyer next to the phone as if waiting for it to ring.

'Dada, waiting for someone to call?' asked Faiz.

'Yes beta, I'm waiting for a phone call from Baray Chacha, I wanted to let him know my arrival date in England so he can pick me up from the airport,' replied Dada.

'Dada, you are leaving too soon,' said Faiz gently. 'Your trips to Pakistan are becoming shorter and shorter. You must move back home now, enough of living in the UK.'

Dada, a handsome man, articulate, even-toned, sharp and with a very dry sense of humour, just smiled as his grandson headed into the house to shower off the July Karachi sweat.

❧

Touring Europe on a food tour, getting professional culinary training and opening a restaurant is an ambitious task and one that requires investment and risk. Maybe in time. But today I have another idea and for that I need Sofia, her enthusiasm, optimism and talent.

Sofia has a gift for writing and my training at the fledging

Indus Valley School of Art and Architecture has managed to hone my art skills. We are thinking of investing our time and expertise in a start-up gift shop specializing in creating innovative, fun and edgy, greeting cards. Dadi says she is willing to bet on us and is lending me some money, and Sofia's Dad is willing to pitch in from his side. All we need is a small office space on rent, commitment and a combination of our talents put to good use.

Our passion has been met with some scepticism by my parents and Sofia's mother, but both of us are convinced that we can make this fly. There is no dearth of talent, good quality paper and independent printing press services in Pakistan. The only thing lacking is the willingness to invest in oneself, and that is something we are willing to change, starting with ourselves.

Both of us are excited and have been brainstorming ideas, so it's only natural that hunger should strike in the middle of the night. We raid Ammi's kitchen. Ammi's trolley is well-laden and is currently decked with naan khatai, sinfully delicious habshi halwa from Multan and fresh savoury snacks from Nimco. We make a fresh pot of chai and roll the trolley on to the verandah, settling in our usual spots and chatting.

Ya Bhai's been of momentous help in guiding us through our business model and has willingly offered his expert business savvy until we may require it. I can't help but wonder whether his interest lies in his fondness for me, or his devotion to Sofia. Funnily enough, even though my affection for Ya Bhai is sibling-like, I feel a little jealous or maybe uncomfortable, with the reality of his infatuation with Sofia.

Why that is, I do not fully understand. I do realize that if I allow it to fester for too long I may spoil my relationship with the both of them, and also jeopardize my new business venture. Therefore, I decide to cap my newfound discomfort, at least for now, until I can address it to Dadi at an opportune time and understand the crux of the issue.

I pick up a naan khatai from the trolley and take a bite, it crumbles and I collect flakes from my plate, make a little morsel and put it in my mouth. Its sugary floury texture has me hooked and I aim for a second helping. Sofia waves a finger at me, 'You know your weakness for biscuits, stop now. If you have a second one you'll have five in a row and will skip breakfast and lunch tomorrow, going straight to dinner. It will mess your entire day up. It's all about portion control and mind control; take control of both.' I can't help but feel shallow and reprimand myself, look at Sofia with her sincerity to me, and me with my recent insincere thoughts of her.

Come lunchtime, I sit down with Dadi and talk about my discomfort at the thought of Ya Bhai and Sofia falling into a relationship, and strangely enough she brushes it aside, 'It's normal, these are two people you care about deeply. They both give you undivided attention. If they fall in love and marry you're scared of becoming second best. So what you feel is natural, but if you think there is a chance they can build a home together, encourage them.'

She opens it up further, 'When you felt their getting together was unrealistic, you encouraged them to get to know each other. Now that there's a real possibility, you are getting cold feet. Yahya and Sofia, both have a good head on their shoulders, and if they are, or are not compatible, they must discover so on their own terms. You must not allow your mind to make negative judgements about their togetherness, and then justify those judgements as being right just because you care about them. You do not know what's best for them, even if you think you do in this moment. Beta, this is not worth losing sleep over. Think about what I have said, you'll feel better about it by the morning.'

Mulling over the love story of my two best friends is a challenge, but in the meantime there is always delicious lamb sajji to alleviate the anxiety, and on queue Jalal walks into the verandah pushing a trolley laden with delicious lunch providing a perfect distraction.

The top tier of the trolley hosts a delicious platter of sajji, stuffed with rice, pomegranate and raisins exuding sweet savoury aroma. The verandah basks in the delicious flowery scent of fruit and lamb, intermixed with the fragrance of the blossoms in the garden. I hear my stomach growl, the delectable scent is playing havoc with my overly sensitive senses and mindless with hunger I serve myself lunch. Sliced boiled eggs serve as a delicious garnish making a great companion to the meat and mildly flavoured rice. I grab a plate and make myself a delicious portion of meat, boiled eggs and baked cauliflower. Thank God for the 20 grams of cauliflower carbs allowed in the induction phase of the Atkins diet.

My delicious plate is ready, and in that moment I decide to concentrate on the flavours of my scrumptious lunch and shut out the noise in the background. I briefly glance at the occupants of the verandah—Sameer, Dadi, Nasreen Phuppo and her daughter, Iffat. Somehow the family and extended family had managed to congregate without my noticing it. I close my eyes and savour the taste of the lamb, basic, rustic, authentic and melt-in-the-mouth tender. My mother follows a centuries-old traditional recipe that according to family legend, came into our clan as a wedding gift.

It was the coming of a Balouchi bride into my mother's side of the family that introduced the authentic sajji as we taste it today. She is said to have belonged to a family of warriors who rode from the open spaces of Makran into Hindustan with the army of Humayun. I don't believe the story, but I certainly believe in the goodness of the sajji.

Tender and young lamb meat lovingly rubbed in salt and

cooked in its own juices to succulence. The artistry is medieval—there is no use of extra spices or marinades, the whole lamb is slowly seduced by the indirect heat of the flame, caressing, loving, stroking, teasing, until the meat is ready to fall off the bone eager to surrender, much like a woman in love.

Did the Balouchi bride feel like a woman in love, I wonder. What was her wedding like? Sajji must have been served at her wedding. Did she fall into the arms of my great uncle, centuries removed, with resistance or with abandon?

I hear laughter in the background, and Iffat wants to know, 'Has the glorious monsoon and taste of sajji taken you back to your Balouchi Mami's wedding?' Iffat is sweet as sugar, sharp as lemon and with a dash of sea salt in homemade butter.

'Yes!' I laugh. 'I was thinking about the sajji recipe and that took me to how it came into our family. Maybe Balouchi Mami actually brought the recipe along with her dowry?' Hearing me speak both of us fell about laughing. Iffat began to describe the wedding as Sameer volunteered to play the part of the groom, and I played the part of the groom's mother. And a fantastic time we had, eating, laughing, and playing out all the drama that must have gone on at that sixteenth-century wedding.

Did those ancestors ever exist? Did they live their lives with the same passions as we do today? The history of food and how it travels regions and conjoins ethnicities fascinates me so much, and the way it connects families and strangers.

She plays the part with unabashed sweet abandon,
Many centuries lost, time mirrors untamed passion,
The sensuous journey of feast remains,
Subtle romance and traditions, the essence of the East maintains.

∽

My hope is to understand the foods of Pakistan and the passions they evoke; it is through art and history that we encapsulate their glorious journey. It is a love story I want to understand, but Dadi insists it's not to be understood, but felt. She says my hours in the kitchen, evocative food sketches, passion for trying to document family recipes, love for searching for unique Pakistani foods and the family stories behind them will lead me to my answers. I could spend entire days sketching people celebrating around food, cooking it, eating it, feeding it, enjoying it.

What is it about food that excites us so much? Is it the taste, the aroma, the pleasure it brings to the palate and the plate, the flavour of the spices and their connection to the subcontinent, or the stories that each dish brings with it?

Food brings us the past and tells us unheard stories as it journeys through time.

Why is it that certain regions and ethnicities prefer rice to wheat? Why are certain foods considered to have a cooling effect in the summer, while others produce warmth in the human body during the winter freeze? And the untold tales of sensuous feasts playing aphrodisiac; the exciting chronicles of passion, celebration and sumptuous eats and drinks.

Dadi is of the opinion that to understand the journey of desi food I need to pay closer attention to the tools that have already been provided to me. She insists that to understand desi food, one does not need to be a professional chef, just a mother who cooks for her family—the best kind of chef.

It is fascinating to me how Dadi insists that a woman's passion and commitment to cooking for her family is her greatest testament to the love she feels for them. The yakhni she makes when her daughter has a cold, the paratha she makes for her little son to nourish his growing body, the khichri she serves ageing parents, the cup of chai she shares with her brothers, sisters and friends and the food she lovingly prepares for her man is a sensuous love story, forever tangible.

'The way to a man's heart is through his stomach. Have you ever heard suggested that the way to a man's heart is in bedding him? No, never,' says Dadi.

I have never heard food and its relationship with people being so described. It makes our relationships with each other, and particularly with those we love, almost tangible and alive. Needless to say, this wonderful exchange with Dadi has left me further confused. Should I go to Italy on a food tour, or just stay on in Pakistan and understand my relationship with food through the people that surround me?

I think of my trip to Fahmeeda Auntie's house, the Palla fish she fed us, the discussion that ensued over the meal and how I have managed to maintain relationships with all the people who travelled with me on that wonderful trip a few years ago. I remember making a promise to return to interior Sindh and pay a visit to the mausoleum of the many Sufi saints and dervishes who lie buried in the province and in other parts of the subcontinent. Somehow I have not managed to keep to my promise, but certainly intend to.

I find myself alone on the verandah. For once the surroundings are serene and the only sound I hear is that of an occasional car or motorbike passing. I rest my head on the chair and start rocking, the gentle motion, soothing, and I find myself day-dreaming. My mind wanders to a time when I was a chubby little girl and eating was uncomplicated. There was no distinction between carbs, protein, juicing, Atkins, too much fat, too much sugar, too much fried, and too much me. I miss the times when I could eat without measuring. There was never any counting of portions, how many biscuits I ate and how many slices of pound cake were chowed down.

I vividly remember our driver used to purchase large bags of biscuits from the Peek Freans Factory in Karachi. The genius idea of the biscuit makers was to package broken baked biscuits into large clear bags and sell them by weight. Broken biscuits could not be sold at supermarkets and were, therefore, packaged and sold at a much cheaper price to the factory workers, making biscuit-eating affordable for those who made them and for their families.

Since I bonded ragingly well with the hired help, our driver, Hanif, informed me about this cheap biscuit acquisition deal. He would get a ten-pound bag of biscuits. I still remember the girth of the bag, it was a body bag of baked delight in a variety of flavours; Marie, chocolate sandwich Bourbon, vanilla sandwich, plain chocolate and plain vanilla.

Hanif would carry the bag home and share half the bag with me for half the price, taking the other half for his children. I would sneak the ten-pound bag into my room, lock my room door, empty the entire bag of broken biscuits onto old newspaper, and divide the batch into two equal portions. I distinctly remember placing the few whole unbroken biscuits in Hanif's pile, so that his children could dance in delight when they stumbled upon one, much like me.

Once the portions were divided, I weighed them on my weighing scale for equal measure, stored my portion in an empty Mackintosh tin container, hid it in my cupboard, returned Hanif's stash to him, paid him for his discretion and the goods, and merrily went about my business.

Each time I watch a rerun of Miami Vice with a drug deal unfolding and hands exchanging cash and goods, I'm reminded of the good old days of exchanging cash and goods too.

In retrospect, it was the stash of biscuits and the carb and sugar-fest at home that led to my excessive weight gain. Ammi loved baking, there was always a freshly fried platter of sugar doughnuts, delicious baked pound cake, lemon tarts, pinwheel biscuits and egg pudding for an anytime snack. And to appease the savoury craving there were large chunks of tender roast beef soaked in gravy, leftover murgh mussallam, sajji and roast raan to be sandwiched for in-between snacking.

As a young teenager I remember stealing meat from the fridge. The way I did this was to grab a glass and then pull out a bottle of water from the fridge, grabbing a hunk of meat with my left hand. I was caught periodically, because I would forget to put the bottle back in the fridge. And whoever opened the fridge to put it back, would spot the missing hunk. They kept an eye out for my pilfering.

Chilled bottles of water were intrinsic to our daily survival. Karachi humidity could turn a chilled bottle of anything lukewarm within minutes. Those days we used only glass bottles and they took time to chill in the fridge. Besides, there were so many of us and we ran through so many bottles in a day that the bottle rack in the fridge (up to five bottles at a time) was always kept full. Anybody who left a bottle out was pulled up.

My dad liked to buy unique glass bottles and would wave in the batley paperwalla onto our front car porch, and negotiate the prices of the prettiest bottles, invariably empty wine bottles, with him. The bottles were then washed and slipped into a large pot of boiling water to remove all traces of alcohol, cooled down, filled with drinking water and stored in the fridge, and then I would come along and waste a perfectly chilled bottle for a handful of meat. Imagine Jalal's and Ammi's frustration during peak summer season when five bottles lay sitting on the counter and none in the fridge.

The gluttony began as I aged into double digits and by age

eleven I was a professional glutton smooth at stealing food, excellent at lying when accused and a champion at solitary eating. Every afternoon after a hearty lunch I would gather my school bag and head to my room pretending to do my homework, but carry on eating instead. Solitary indulgence, the hallmark of all dependencies, invariably begins as a dismissive bad habit, but converts to complete addiction, a love affair with an obsession we call a failing.

Now, some ten years later, I realize that solitary eating is a loyal companion to victims of obesity, and cheers them on to extreme weight gain. As I moved from simple double digits to my early teens, I realized the onset and pressures of external beauty. Each time I heard someone talk about a pretty girl, I would go to my room and stuff my face with broken biscuits, much like my spirit.

Was there any unbroken, undamaged biscuit in the tin box? No.

From the outside the box was colourful to look at, noisy when opened and fun to hangout with; once opened, the contents of the box were sweet and delicious, but broken and incomplete. The overall picture was much like me, a combination of round, fun, noticeable, sweet, but somewhat damaged from the inside.

Apparently all was pretty as a picture with my life, there was nothing obviously lacking, but under the layers, lurking in the shadows were insecurities that kept nagging, making me feel faulty. Maybe it was my height, mild acne, the fact that I was not very good at sports, that my hands and feet were not very attractive, that I was a below average student, and later my progressive weight gain.

Despite my lacking all of the above but weight, I was generally a happy child, unless reminded of my insecurities. Any reminder resulted in delicious gluttony until I felt better and stopped, only for the cycle to begin all over again when someone else mentioned any or all of these sore points.

My older brother, Nadir, was everything I was not, and he made sure I witnessed his success consistently. Like most older siblings he knew how to push my parents' buttons, and would usually highlight my failings when I was most vulnerable. Being over-zealous, I would get into trouble for retaliating with a few choice words, while he would cunningly remain oh-so-calm as I grew agitated, and he would invariably get away with it. Abbu mostly focused on my failings, yelling at what I did (or failed to do) and at what I had become, but never understood the journey that took me to that point.

For instance, I would get a bad grade and he would focus on the bad grade, but never on why I got it. I don't think he even thought about it that way—maybe I wasn't as intelligent as Nadir; maybe I didn't study as much as Nadir. Maybe nobody asked a little girl if she had finished her homework, nobody checked it for errors, but yelled at her for bringing home failed tests, and then questioned her intelligence.

During that time my one true champion was food. When people started commenting on my weight, each time I ate; solitary eating became my knight in shining armour. Food never questioned me, it never judged, it never indulged my despondence on my appearance, instead it made me happy, and happiness is all a little girl wants.

The cycle went on, my grades did not improve, my weight kept piling on and Ammi kept pounding me emotionally, until that long-gone day on the beach when everything changed and we started our journey home together, one to connect with a dead mother, and the other to connect with a living one.

∾

Failed arrangement

'Why Dadi? Spare me today, I promise to go with you tomorrow. Why can't we go tomorrow?' I ask, desperate to be excused from accompanying Dadi to Nasreen Phuppo's house.

'Nasreen bought new furniture for the drawing room. I want to surprise her with these cushion covers I made to match. You go for a walk every evening. Can't you skip one day? Are you meeting someone at the park?' Dadi asks, her eyes suspiciously amused and her tone almost merry at the thought of me meeting a secret admirer.

'Dadi, what is wrong with you? I'm not having clandestine meetings in the park, what kind of question is that? I just hate skipping a day of exercise, and if I want to meet someone I'll invite them home, not go behind anyone's back,' I say laughing, almost challenging myself to go out and start meeting someone on the sly.

'Okay, and when I pass on, when I'm no more,' she sighs deeply, 'you can think about today and the choice you made,' says Dadi. She certainly knows how to get her stubborn old way.

'You are such an emotional blackmailer!' I say rolling my eyes, and storm off to get my dupatta.

We arrive at Phuppo's and walk into a drawing room decorated with new furniture and guests. There is an older couple, approximately my parents' age with their son, serving themselves from a trolley laden with chai and lavish accompaniments. The young gentleman is dressed sharp, is well-spoken and pleasant looking, and is merrily chatting me up. I find myself answering questions and get rather uncomfortable with the whole exchange. Expectedly, another family arrives with their daughter dressed in her Sunday best. She gives me a rather cold smile, is introduced to the boy, Moeed Mir, and finds a spot next to him. I get it. Nasreen

Phuppo is playing matchmaker. If Moeed and this girl hit it off, and further negotiations go smoothly, they'll be married off.

To my chagrin, Moeed Mir abandons the girl and finds his way back to me to continue his discussion from where we left off. I eye his plate and his obvious aversion to all things meat and sweet, and my disinterest goes up a notch.

'I'm training to be a doctor and am currently doing my house job. What about you?' he asks.

'Oh, I just started my own business. I design greeting cards and my company goes by the name "Musings Over a Cup of Tea",' I reply, wanting to end the game of twenty questions.

'Oh, so you are a writer too, that's great. I'm thinking of quitting medicine and pursuing a career in journalism,' he says rather enthusiastically.

'No, I'm not a journalist, or a writer. I'm an artist, and I leave the writing to my creative writing department, that's not my forte,' and I get up to get a cup of chai from the trolley so I can politely escape and park myself in the dining room, adjacent to the drawing room.

'Did you do your schooling here?' Moeed asks, and I spot Dadi looking my way from across the room, amused at the way the evening is unfolding. I make my way to her. Incorrigible Dadi, I could have gone for my evening walk, Moeed and what's-her-name could have made eyes at each other and gotten married.

We finally head home and Dadi gloats to Ammi and a very distressed looking Salma Khala. 'Mark my words, before the end of this evening we'll have a marriage proposal for you. That Moeed fellow, he looked very interested and his mother asked so many questions about you.'

'Dadi!' I am aghast.

However, experience is the best pundit and half an hour

later the phone rings solidifying Dadi's status as the household soothsayer. I laugh perplexed, embarrassed and guilty, and feel sad for the girl. She dolled up to meet Moeed. Maybe she had seen a photograph of him and was excited about a dialogue and I, unintentionally, stole that from her, changing the course of both their lives, possibly forever. Even prospective marriages are taken to the heart here.

Dadi is excited and wants to know if I am ready that he be invited to the house.

I find myself shaking my head and mouthing a big NO.

'Dadi I have plans with someone else, but first I have to find him and then bring him home.'

～

MURGH MUSSALLAM

In my observation, hosts serving a whole chicken at lavish or intimate dinners always call it roast chicken and never murgh mussallam, and now I understand why. Because it is not and never was, the royal murgh mussallam. The spices were a tad western, boiled eggs were never an accompaniment, and it was never stuffed with lamb keema (lamb mince), as in the original royal recipe.

In other words, I have enjoyed a fine meal of roast chicken countless times, but never murgh mussallam in the true sense, as referred to by the Mughals of centuries past.

Ingredients
1 whole chicken (approx. 3lb)
2 green chillies
10 to 15 cloves of garlic

½ inch piece of ginger
1 tsp garam masala powder
A pinch of turmeric powder
8 oz yogurt
1 tsp red chilli powder
Whole garam masala (4 to 6 brown cardamom pods, 8 to 10 cloves, 1 piece cinnamon, 8 to 10 peppercorns)
1 tsp cumin seeds
2 tsp coriander seeds
15 almonds
2 to 4 oz oil (or to taste)
2 large onions
Salt to taste
2 to 4 oz water
Freshly chopped coriander for garnish

Method

Blend ginger, garlic, yogurt, green chillies, salt, ½ tsp red chilli powder, turmeric and garam masala powder into a thick marinade for the chicken. Marinate whole chicken, spreading masala inside the cavity and let it rest in the fridge for 4 to 5 hours.

Roast whole garam masala, cumin and coriander seeds and almonds and set these whole roasted spices aside.

In a large heavy pan, or pot, heat oil and fry thinly sliced onions until golden brown. Remove the now golden brown onions from the pan and add to the whole roasted spices that have been set aside. Use blender to make a paste of the onions and whole roasted spices, add a little water if required.

In the same pan used for frying the onions, braise the marinated whole chicken for a few minutes (saving the marinade for later use), then remove and set aside.

In the same pan heat a little oil and fry the paste of the onions and whole roasted spices on high heat, adding the rest of the red chilli powder, marinade, and salt if required. Fry on high heat for a few minutes, then add the whole chicken and water, seal the lid, and cook on medium heat. Cook for 15 to 20 minutes on one side, and 10 to 15 on the other.

Once the meat is tender, set in a platter, pouring the masala on the top and sides, and garnish with greens. Serve with a side of your favourite vegetables and boiled eggs, hot naan and raita.

I served it with a side of shallow fried peas, tomatoes, potatoes and bell peppers. Truly a delectable meal, enjoy.

♦

NAMKEEN GOSHT

Ammi makes the most delicious namkeen gosht, but only once a year at Bakr Eid (Eid-ul-Azha), hence it truly is an Eid-to-Eid fare. Each year I beg and plead and Ammi says, 'Bakr Eid is just around the corner.'

And my response, 'Ammi it's six months away,' is always met with a promise of, 'I'll make it tomorrow', and tomorrow always comes annually at Bakr Eid. It's wonderful how precious memories and delicious food are linked, surely we all have wonderful memories from when parents and grandparents indulged us, pampering us with favourite foods; where the main ingredient was a bucket load of TLC, more commonly known as tender loving care.

We can safely say that mutton is a favourite with the mountain people, where the consumption of meat is a way of combating the rigorous weather and terrain; keeping them strong, warm and warrior-like. Its tender melt-in-the-mouth texture, thanks to slow cooking and minimum use of ingredients, makes namkeen gosht an all-time favourite with meat lovers.

What else makes namkeen gosht such a hit?

The flavour and tender bite of meat, generally cooked after being freshly slaughtered, are not lost in a multitude of spices and vegetables. The main ingredients of this dish are salt, ginger and pepper, and they give the dish a subtle flavour that is overwhelmingly meaty.

Historically speaking, lamb and mutton have always been favoured meats in South Asia, the Middle East, Central Asia, and the Mediterranean. Maybe it was the availability of the animal, its size, the fact that it was not a predator, or that its meat is deliciously tender and juicy—whatever the reason, it became the target of choice when hunting for a quick and easy dinner.

My two favourites every Eid-ul-Azha are namkeen gosht made by my mother with the fresh meat of the *qurbani ka bakra* (sacrificed goat), and the special karahi gosht, made by my father.

Namkeen gosht is deliciously rustic and hearty. It is traditionally made with small cubes of lamb or goat cooked in ginger, salt, black pepper and/or green chillies, and preferably animal fat. The fresh meat provides the fat base for the cooking, and it is most delicious when served with a side of hot naan, lemon wedges and sliced onions.

Ingredients

2 lb goat leg, cut in small cubes

1 ½ to 2 tbsp freshly chopped ginger

½ to 1 freshly diced tomato

4 to 5 green chillies slit lengthwise (optional, but preferable, this gives it a real kick)

Salt to taste

Oil ¼ to ½ cup, but with freshly slaughtered meat the animal fat should suffice

Method

Heat oil in heavy-lidded wok. Fry green chillies and ginger for a minute, add meat, salt, tomato and black pepper, and stir on high heat for a few minutes until the heat causes the meat to release juices. Seal pot with lid and simmer on low to medium heat for a few minutes, turning the heat to low and cook until meat is tender and falling off the bone. The meat juices gradually steam and evaporate, sealing in the juices, and slow cooking the meat to perfection. Avoid adding water if possible, but if need arises add a little water to the cooking process.

Serve with naan, lemon wedges and sliced onions.

Chapter 4

Lahore

Subtle Flavours of Regale, Regality and Romance

While reading the daily *Dawn*, I came across an article about a Food Anthropologist with expertise in the cuisines of the subcontinent, and a start-up food-centric business, touring the cities of Pakistan. The touring company is called Food Stories Global and markets its touring product as a link to the food heritage of the subcontinent, for foodies and professional chefs alike. The concept is brilliant and caters to all interested in food and its history. Food Stories Global prides itself in researching the foods of a particular region, its history, evolution, cultural significance, links to the inhabitants, traditions behind serving a particular food to family and friends, and ends the tutorial with a tasting of regional foods.

I shelve the idea of going to Italy and instead decide to embark on this food journey through Pakistan. However, I have to get my parents' permission first. Maybe if I could convince Sofia to come with me on Food Stories Global's fast-approaching Lahore Tour that would persuade Ya Bhai to come along, which would induce Nadir and Sameer to tag along, thus completing the quorum and ensuring permission was granted?

To get the three guys to agree I would have to ensure the trio assumed the idea came from them. That's the only way this was going to work. Pakistan is still very much a patriarchal society;

however, mindsets are changing, slowly but surely.

And so, I take myself off to B. Bees, which Ya Bhai has managed to turn into one of the trendiest restaurants in the city—it's *the* hangout now. Converting Pakistan's burger-eating youth to the biryani cause was no mean feat. Biryani, until B. Bees, was never considered sophisticated eating; and there are countless unsophisticated ways to eat biryani in Pakistan.

Pakistan devours biryani at street corners, wolfs it down in *langars* at *mazaars*, eats it out of takeaway plastic bags, serves it up as one among many sumptuous items at lavish weddings, or the only item at humble one-dish weddings—biryani holds its own in Pakistan.

And B. Bees has made it upmarket. The walls in the main dining area are painted in shades of moss green with a beige border running at the top and base; the back wall facing the entrance boasts bold striking graffiti art—portraits and quotations of contemporary revolutionary artists. Seating capacity has doubled since Ya Bhai bought the pharmacy next door. Round teak tables with teak chairs upholstered in moss green, pale yellow and tangerine fill the large room; there's enough room between tables for movement and privacy. I casually occupy my favourite spot in the far right corner, farthest from the entrance with the best vantage point.

As usual, the dining room is packed to capacity, with biryani servings floating in and empty plates floating out. Humming to the background beat of 'Bamboleo', by the Gypsy Kings, I take out the folded newspaper from my purse and reread the article. Going on a food tour of Lahore is an exciting prospect, and I'm fairly convinced that getting the three boys on my side will not be difficult, but I know it won't be so easy with Sofia. Her recent break up with Zahid means she's not going to see anything great about going on the trip unless I convince her to view Ya Bhai as a candidate for romance.

What's not to like about Ya Bhai? I find myself making a list of his positives on the back of a takeaway menu on the table.

1. In his late twenties.
2. Only child—lion's share of inheritance, one has to weigh these things, we may not be the Mughals i.e., inheriting empires, but neither are we cane-furniture makers.
3. Masters in Business Administration, and owns and runs the very successful B. Bees.
4. Hardworking, intelligent and tenacious.
5. Very well-spoken; does not have a strong Memoni accent like Tayajee Tyyab.
6. 5 feet 6 inches in height, he could be taller, but who am I to complain at 5 feet 1 inch.
7. Lives in Karachi Development Authority.
8. Decent guy, a little nerdy, but certainly a pleasant looking nerd, with a full head of hair, glasses, sharp eyes and an angular nose. Yup, he's cute, maybe nerd cute.
9. He wants to get married.
10. Already in love with prospect.

My list compiled I stuff it into my purse and stare blankly ahead, soaking in the activity and waiting for Sofia to show. The front door swings open and Sofia enters, pretty, scattered and in a rush, always in a rush.

~

The Knight of the crescent

Faiz parks his Honda Civic by the curbside outside B. Bees, staying seated for a minute to collect his thoughts. It is a hot, humid day with ominous clouds that look ready to burst and he plans to pick up a biryani, head home and wrap up a project he's working on, before Karachi Electric Supply Corp. quits on him.

He has worked countless nights in the dark under battery-operated lamplights and the flickering glow of candles; *if only I managed my time a little better*, he thinks—*go to work on time, come home a little earlier, start squash earlier, eat dinner with the family and sleep at a decent hour, then maybe life would be a little more organized.*

But Faiz is Faiz, never pre-plans; as he puts it, 'life is to be lived in the moment.'

He enters B. Bees and looks idly around, his gaze falling on a pale-skinned girl with long dark hair and slender arms. She's wearing a red outfit and sitting alone, writing. She pauses for a moment and as though conscious of his gaze, looks up. Delicately arched eyebrows, dark eyes, a small round face with a straight nose and striking red lips. Suddenly she smiles and just as he's about to smile back, a tall girl walks past him to greet the girl in crimson. And just as suddenly the girls are walking toward the door, and the vision in red drops a crumpled bit of paper by Faiz as she walks out.

He almost follows her through the door, but the receptionist tells him his biryani order is ready. He picks up a couple of attractive moss-green boxes with large black lettering on the top right corner reading B. Bees, and walks to his car, lingering inside hoping to catch another glimpse of red.

Later that night, he stands at his drawing board drafting and mapping his latest project. The recently acquired government tender his senior partners bid on, and won, will aid in the construction of the Ghazi Barotha Hydropower project on the River Indus near the city of Attock, Punjab. It is an exciting governmental project with social and environmental implications. Faiz is busy trying to calculate the water-flow impact on the diverted river flowing downstream through Tarbela Dam into the city of Ghazi, then through the powerhouse before flowing back to the Indus. Despite his passion for his work, his concentration is low, and he finally walks away from the drawing board, slumps on to the purple beanbag and presses the play button on the stereo remote. 'Faithfully' by *Journey*: he should have gone to their concert in his college days at Caltech, but maybe another time.

He rests his head on the wall behind, closes his eyes and pulls a cushion to his chest, playing hide and seek with slumber until he falls asleep.

Faiz dreamt beautiful dreams that night. Dreams of gardens and song, hills and colours, breeze and moss green, and the afterglow of red. Beautiful blankets of red silk caressing him, stroking him, embracing him, wrapping him in softness, soaking him in everlasting fragrance and colour. Faiz smiled in his sleep and pulled the red blanket closer.

> *She passes ever so gently, caressing the heart so close,*
> *Sprinkling hues of crimson red, sparkling with yellow gold,*
> *Tales of passion laced in feast have begun once again,*
> *Time is the only witness, joy the only game.*

Shalimar Gardens, Lahore

I stood in the centre of the lavish garden, amidst lush blossoms, thick foliage, orange, mango, apple and apricot trees, on an expanse of green grass surrounded by flittering butterflies. I could hear the dhol being played at a distance, beating out the rhythm of welcome. It was the coming of a *baraat*. I slipped my feet out of my slippers, curling my toes into the moist grass and soaked in the scent of the garden, drunk on the magnificence of the blue canvas hosting orange, pink and yellow hues of the setting sun. And then, I stretched my arms sideways and started spinning, my white chiffon dupatta spinning. I spun to the sound of bangles and dhol, spun round and round, almost like in a *sema*, and suddenly stopped. My world whirling, laughing, I fell to the ground and lay on the grass, eyes closed momentarily and opened them to the twirling shadows of dancing dervishes everywhere, wearing colours, hair flying, and joined them reeling and wheeling and circling in the unending delight of the moment.

The sound of the dhol became louder, as did the sound of dancing feet and all the dancers suddenly broke into a *luddi*. We all clapped in unison, moved our feet in sync and maintained a steady rhythm to the sound of the drum, the dhol. In my head, or maybe somewhere in another time, I heard a rendition of 'Chaap Tilak', undeniably Amir Khusro at his best; the song kept playing over and over in my head, and suddenly the awareness of how blessed I was to be in that moment, to be alive and breathing dawned on me.

Sofia, Sameer and I fell laughing onto the grass as did the other tourists who had joined us in a moment of spontaneity. Rarely does the coming together of variables brings about a perfect moment: a confluence of music, masti, moon and mehfil playing magic, and we let the moment take charge, handing the reins of pragmatism to Nadir and Yahya who, exasperated and amused at us three, signalled their departure from the Mughal structure pondering the magnificence of the gardens at its zenith and the echo of glory lost to time.

> *The brilliance of the gardens somewhat remains,*
> *She danced once before, almost the same,*

The grass was a carpet, lush and green,
Tune seduced her aura, timeless poetry made her forever queen.

~

Old city, Lahore

What most consider trivial I consider impactful; food, friendship, family, faith, feelings of love and health. These Simple Six, if practised well and in balance, form the foundation of a life well-spent. And none of them requires much money to create a melodiously harmonious life; all they require is a dose of sincerity, devotion, understanding and balance.

Happiness is based in the simple, and simplicity, as I've come to understand is very hard to achieve, while complicated is very easy. I hear people throw around the phrase, 'she's so simple, or he's so simple,' and it's almost always used with implied condescension.

Why?

If only they understood that sages fathom the simple only after appreciating the wisdom in it. They absorb its depth, peel its layers, and realize the uncomplicated in its purest and most elevated form, through contentment and peace.

Sofia and I sat talking late last night and pondered the wisdom of simple emotions and the perils of complicated ones. We are staying at Taya Abbu Tanveer's house in Lahore and sharing a room, as are Ya Bhai, Nadir and Sameer. Taya Abbu Tanveer is my father's older brother. He's wonderfully warm and a male version of my Dadi; he's big hearted, generous and has the best sense of humour, much like his wife, Rehana Tai. The five of us showed up at Rehana Tai's house at a day's notice and were warmly welcomed.

Entertaining family and friends, overnight guests or otherwise, is the mark of South Asian hospitality.

It's akin to the ways of the English aristocracy of the centuries past, either they learnt this tradition from the people of the subcontinent when they came to colonize it, or we learnt it from them. Regardless it's a tradition that has stayed behind and forms the backbone of South Asian culture. Children are nurtured in this long-established custom and make true the saying 'it takes a village to raise a child'. Through this upbringing they learn 'lihaaz', a word that has no direct English translation and is a purely South Asian concept, and can only be defined vaguely as 'respectful consideration for peers, elders and youth, where a deliberate biting of the tongue or curbed reaction, is much preferred to an assertive retort.'

Standing in the central courtyard of Haveli Niazbagh I ponder on the discussion of last night. Rehana Tai may have been right in trying to convince Sofia and me that bygone days were much simpler. My argument to her was that all generations believe that their ancestors led a simpler life and felt simpler emotions, when, in fact, being simple is a state of mind and being, and not an outcome of the times people live in. Through the course of the discussion we agreed that both beliefs hold true. Newer innovations accompanying each generation bring about convenience, but in essence also nibble away the cause of simple living and a simple mindset. Therefore, each generation assumes that the one before them was simpler, and so both arguments run parallel to a degree.

Haveli Niazbagh speaks of a time when large noble families lived in sprawling majestic homes, raised children together, had meals together and focused on simpler emotions, and Food Stories Global has arranged a special evening to honour the bygone days with a delicious feast laced in flavours of authentic Lahori cuisine.

The walk to the haveli is delightful, the driver drops us at a bus stop near the Delhi Gate, one of the thirteen historical gates walling in the old city of Lahore, and bids adieu. We meet our group of twenty foodies, waiting at the designated spot to further enjoy Lahore's culinary treasures and set on foot towards the historical Haveli Niazbagh located near Taxali Gate.

Once inside the gates, I am absolutely mesmerized by the bazaar, though it is reminiscent of the narrow bazaars and congested ancient markets in historical cities, yet it has a uniquely South Asian flavour to it. The narrow ancient cobbled streets are a veritable time capsule from the Mughal era. Shops speckle the congested alleyway—earthenware sellers, tea sellers, cloth merchants, spice traders, vegetable vendors, wheat distributors, noise, din, life; and the generations living it for centuries. They call out to me to buy bangles, and I do. I am wearing plain white cotton with Lucknawi embroidery, hence the bangle-seller suggests silver glass bangles, and I go with his suggestion.

Many a silver and golden *zari, dubka, moti* and *sitara* adorned bridal wear is lavishly displayed in the fluorescent white-lit shops, and women window shop, caressing the cloth to check for quality. We pass the Royal Baths, known as the *Shahi Hamam*, which were once grand and lavish; but now I see nothing in the area except a dilapidated government school and a few shops.

Hakim Ansari is said to have built the baths in the year 1634, and they are famed for extravagance in construction and plumbing, much like the royal baths of ancient Turkey and Bath, England. The Shahi Haman seems to have perished, or was maybe deliberately buried under mortar and bricks by the British Raj. They came to erase subcontinental glory from history, unaware that eras can never be erased, only forgotten until a new generation takes birth and searches for the glory of the past, creating a renewed resurgence in cultural pride and heritage.

The journey to Taxali Gate is almost like a history lesson. A local in our group gives us an extempore tour, pointing to the old talkies cinema called Nazir Cinema before Partition, but which now only shows porn. Amir, our makeshift guide, points to the homes of the poet Altaf Hussain Hali and Allama Iqbal. I can't help but wonder what poems they wrote while maintaining residence here and my mind invariably goes to the scandalous happenings at Heera Mandi somewhere in close proximity.

Having recently viewed *The Dancing Girls of Lahore,* a documentary on the infamous Heera Mandi, I was heartbroken to hear the apathy with which the girls talked about the sex trade. A young boy candidly waited outside a room while his mother indulged in her business behind a curtain, his eyes expressionless, voice monotonous and future bleak. Maybe the boy will become an inspirational success story one day and talk about his sordid birth and his rise from it. I smile unwittingly hoping for his success, and ask, 'How far to Haveli Niazbagh?'

'Here it is,' replies our host Mian Habibullah Niaz in a booming voice. An impressive-looking man in his forties, big and tall, wearing a crisp white kameez-shalwar, he welcomes us into the haveli with a quintessentially Punjabi 'jee aaya noon' kind of welcome. I observe his face. He's fair with a square jawline, dark eyes, a Roman nose and an Arab-style beard. I've seen him somewhere, or someone resembling him. Suddenly I feel an elbow in my ribs. 'My God, he's so good looking. Doesn't he look like the Nawab of Junagarh! Now let's find out if his wife is as pretty and deserves him,' exclaims Sofia, rather expectedly.

'Oh Sofia, you love playing with Ya Bhai's feelings, don't you? You know how much he likes you, and still keep messing with his feelings by screaming your devotion to all the Greek gods of the world. But since this one is married he's safe from you,' I reply, pulling her leg.

'No one's safe from me. I like this haveli, and when I like something I sometimes need to have it,' announces Sofia.

Sofia scares me when she gets into one of her moods and I almost don't want Ya Bhai to set his hopes on settling down with her. I love her dearly, but also see her inherent desire for adventure, newness and an almost pathological need to attract male attention. If there is a male in the room, Sofia needs his eyes on her, his ears on her and his focus on her. She'll unwittingly throw her head back and laugh a little louder, smile a little knowingly, and talk a little lustier, and combined with her husky voice and good looks she is irresistible when indulging her carnal instincts.

My male cousins, family friends' sons, and even the neighbour's dog are intrigued by her persona. Interestingly, Nadir enjoys a great platonic relationship with her, maybe because he is much like her and understands her disposition entirely. I regularly walk into the both of them exchanging notes and discussing their latest conquests with intense satisfaction. God, how I love them both, and hate them a little too.

The haveli is absolutely magnificent, a square courtyard housing a central water fountain a few inches raised. A ten- to twelve-foot wide covered boundary of the courtyard leads to a dozen ornately carved, large double doors. Eleven doors are charcoal grey and the twelfth is the central silver door leading to the back of the haveli. All doors lead to rooms opening into the traditional courtyard, the main venue for tonight's lavish reception.

There are almost a hundred people at the reception and the long corridor with the large silver doors is where the tables are laid out for the food to be displayed. There are *diyas* and darbans, spreading light and appetizers, the lamplight glimmers through the *jharokas* creating a magical illumination as the red brick walls glow. I close my eyes to soak in the moment and focus on the beat of the tabla and sitaar, and commend myself on making this journey, somehow aware that this journey will change my world forever. I open my eyes to a tap on my shoulder and see Imran, the owner of Food Stories Global ready to make conversation.

'Are you enjoying yourself Ayesha, what do you think of the venue and ambience?'

'It's perfect,' I said, 'I'm still trying to soak in the magic of the evening. I absolutely loved the walk to Haveli Niazbagh; the old city is steeped in history. The sounds, the smells, the narrow alleyways are magnificent.' Imran nodded in agreement.

'I can't thank you enough for enabling us to experience the cultural heritage of grand Lahore, not to mention the lavish feast I'm waiting to dig into. This haveli is an architectural dream, I have a few questions about the restoration work on it and was hoping you could introduce me to Mrs Habibullah Niaz. Look I got bangles, how entirely cultural of me,' I reply shaking my silver wrists for the *chhun chhun* sound, and laugh at my filmy and almost flirty gesture.

Imran throws his head back laughing, 'Here, let me introduce you to my cousin-in-law, he'll answer your questions. Not that he knows anything about this building, but I have to mingle and think it rude to leave a pretty girl like you alone. Here, meet Faiz. Faiz this is Ayesha.'

The man named Faiz is standing with his back to Imran; he turns and smiles at me customarily as the introductions are made. He's wearing khaki chinos, a pale, checked mustard shirt, and tan loafers. I maintain a nonchalant expression while keenly observing his brown eyes and gelled hair, defined mouth and full bottom lip; on the whole, rather pleasant on the eyes at first glance.

I smile back, curious, interested and intrigued, and watch Imran walk away. There is momentary silence but I find a conversational topic and jump on it, 'How do you like the food tour so far?'

'Oh, I'm not on the food tour. I'm here tonight because I happen to be in Lahore for the week and Imran invited me for dinner this evening. Apparently this is a very happening event, with a surprise to end the evening,' replies Faiz in a precisely modulated and pleasant tone. He asks, 'Are you here on the food tour?'

'I am and it's been quite an experience so far. We've eaten so much wonderfully delicious food on this tour. Food Stories Global makes grand arrangements. The food experiences, history lessons and the hospitality of the people of Lahore have been charming. It's been worth every penny, but don't tell Imran I said that,' I say as both of us chuckle.

I find myself walking to the two-seater swing in the far corner diagonal to the bar, hoping to escape the eyes of my four companions in an effort to maintain my current company. Faiz follows and starts walking with me, and just as suddenly in swoops a pretty woman and whisks him away, much like a hawk ready to break up a destination-bound migration of doves.

Needless to say, male doves don't particularly like migrating, only females do, hence the hawk's timing is perfect. Her high-pitched cackle is rather unpleasant as she whispers something in his ear and pulls him aside. Faiz apologetically flashes me a 'gimme a minute' kind of smile and sails away on the wings of the shrill-voiced woman in a rather tacky hot pink and emerald green outfit. I can't help but frown at the eighties colour combination she is wearing.

I walk to the swing and take centre seat, ensuring little space on my left and right in the hopes of discouraging bored attendees who may want a seat on the swing.

Faiz—my mind wanders to him as do my eyes, and I smile at the thought of Tanveer Taya emphatically describing him as debonair. Each time Taya Abbu sees a handsome man he refers to him as debonair, a word not heard often enough. Debonair, Faiz is for sure; fair, with a pleasant masculine tan, baby brown eyes, a full head of dark brown hair, a slightly snub nose on a somewhat round face. But who is the hot pink lollipop who whisked him away—girlfriend, sister, cousin, fiancé, friend, or maybe his wife?

I hope it's not his wife.

My eyes fall on a very animated Sofia and Nadir next to the dinner table. They seem to be lost in conversation possibly comparing notes on Habibullah Niaz and some girl that Nadir must have met. I hope it's not Mrs Habibullah Niaz that Nadir is animated about. That would be too much of a coincidence and I find my pursed lips curving to smile. Ya Bhai is busy making a business deal with Imran. I see them laughing, probably about B. Bees playing host to Food Stories Global, while the food tours are stationed in Karachi. Ya Bhai has been trying to strike a deal with Imran in the hopes of making the needful happen; I hope it does.

I rest my head back and start swinging, a beautiful night, intoxicating aroma of the food, heady music, sensuous ambience and me. I see a waiter walking towards me with a glass of meethi lassi, and behind him appears Faiz, picking two glasses of lassi off the tray and walking towards me, instead of the waiter. I feel my heart beat a little faster, sit up straight and move to my right. Faiz hands me a glass of lassi and sits on my left, the swing creaks a little in protest, but who's listening.

'What if it breaks?' I quip, eyes wide open in pretend innocence.

'I'll catch you!' he says with laughing eyes. Hearing his response I start giggling uncontrollably, releasing the tension in the moment, but it starts building over again in the next instance.

We start talking and I tell Faiz about my passion for food and food history, and my almost Italian food tour that did not happen,

'Hence I'm here in Lahore touring desi food and sitting on this swing in this gorgeous haveli. If I had my way, I would be in a Tuscan villa eating margarita pizza chatting away with Roberto.'

'Roberto Cavalli?' Faiz says with a straight face and laughing eyes, to my quick repartee.

'Ha ha, that's so funny, NOT!'

'I'm serious, look,' he replies.

'No, you're clever,' I say.

'Okay, I'm seriously clever.'

We find ourselves talking about old Lahore and the multitude of havelis and heritage homes in the area. Faiz mentions that Taxali Gate is named so because the Mughals had stationed the royal mint in this very vicinity, and since the Urdu word for mint is 'taxal', therefore the gate was named Taxali. The mint exists no more, but its memory does, like much in this area. Next we talk about the O.J. Simpson case, and whether Simpson is guilty or not for the double murder of his wife and her lover. We debate the topic for a while and the issue of race comes up, and Faiz emphatically insists, 'Race is always an issue; we'll just have to wait and see what the jury says.'

Lost in conversation we find ourselves at the beautifully spread dinner table. Sameer walks up from behind me and drapes his arm around my shoulder, 'Hey Ash, what's happening, kahan thi, where were you?'

'Where were you?' I respond. 'I've seen the other three cropping up on the courtyard once in a while, but you I have not seen. Were you smoking weed in the *galli*?'

'Are you crazy Ash, Spanish inquisition or what?'

'Faiz, meet my younger brother Sameer, and he does not smoke weed. Hopefully. I was only teasing him.'

The men exchange niceties as I turn my attention to the lavishly laid banquet table and find myself humming, 'What a Wonderful World' by Louis Armstrong. The aroma emanating from the table is intoxicating and I can almost taste the savoury payaa, pulao, shami kabab, chikar cholay, murgh mussallam, Lahori fish, raan roast, namkeen gosht, four kinds of salads including kachumber, a variety of naan and sabzi, raita, achar and murabaay.

The luxurious ivory silk table cover plays a perfect backdrop to the extravagant display of food and drink. Each dinner entrée is set in intricately carved platters and bowls of German silver, sparkling and spotless, and garnished with greens from the herb garden. The chutneys and achar are displayed in oblong gravy boat dishes matching the large silver platters, and the bready aroma of freshly baked naan is a perfect moment to break bread. Thus we begin dinner.

I pile my plate with mutton pulao and shami kabab and make my way to the table where Sofia and the rest of the gang are seated. The table is large enough to seat twenty-four people and is in the formal dining area inside the haveli. Faiz seems busy socializing while making a dinner plate and I find myself walking away. I don't want to seem presumptuous, but if I stayed on, it might look as though we were obligated to walk away together, since we had walked to the dinner table together.

I sit at the far end of the table admiring the ornately decorated dining room. China cabinets display beautiful crockery, a flat table with a glass lid flamboyantly showcases silver- and gold-plated cutlery, tall paintings exhibiting artwork, embellished swords and daggers hanging on the walls and lamplight and candles casting shadows that play hide and seek with each other.

The ambience is traditionally grand, and I can't help but think of another time, maybe centuries ago, when a girl met a charming man over a splendid meal and was intrigued by him. I catch Sofia's eyes, she gives me a questioning glance and I shrug it off flippantly.

I see her glaring back, she wants to know about Faiz ASAP. I smile and wave at her and decide to focus on my dinner plate instead.

No carbs this month so why does my plate have only rice, and that too pulao. I fleetingly flirt with the idea of changing my plate, but the effervescent pulao beckons and I willingly surrender.

Why is it so easy to surrender to beautiful flavours?

Why are delicious foods so irresistible? They play havoc with the body but we still love them, whether meetha, *khatta* or namkeen. Dadi often draws a parallel between love and food, and brazenly implies that food, love, music, dance, passion and sex are co-related.

My weight loss may have been a result of yo-yo dieting, starvation and denial of essential nutrients to the body, but Dadi insists that the only way to attain a balanced body is through learning to appreciate all kinds of foods, eating them in proportion and sharing them with others and lovers.

Dadi was, and still is a quintessential hostess. She passionately talks about her love story with my grandfather and how he fell in love with her because of her passion for cooking. And each time she tries to convince me of having a more balanced diet, she says, 'The journey of life is fervent. All one needs is a few friends, a food fetish, a fine fellow, a fair fortune and fitness of family and self; everything else is just fluff.'

And to celebrate Dadi's food fetish I make a beeline for the dessert table. Once outside, my eyes search for a mustard shirt, but it's nowhere to be found. Maybe I'll see him again; he did say he lives in Karachi and was here only for a week. The dessert table is laden with mustard hues, chanay ke daal ka halwa, shahi tukray, besan mithai and patheesa, but no sighting of the mustard shirt. Apparently, the sweetest of all the mustard coloured desserts seems to be missing from the table. Invariably I settle for chanay ke daal ka halwa, an otherwise favourite dessert of mine.

Somewhere from the back of the haveli I hear music and the sound of *payal*. Lost in thought, I become aware that the courtyard is almost empty. It's me and a few other people, who also seem to be walking towards the sound of music.

The duo playing the sitaar and tabla seem to be missing from the courtyard and have converted to a full orchestra from what I can hear. The silver glass bangles are sprinkling glitter on my clothes and bare arms and I touch my cheek, transferring sparkle to my face and hair too. Unsuccessfully brushing the silver dust off my white sleeveless kurta, I walk to the swing and commend my family for eagerly listening to the *sham-e-ghazal* inside. And then I hear her.

> *Chaap tilak sab cheeni ray mosay naina milaikay*
> *Baat agam keh deeni ray mosay naina milaikay*
> *Prem bhatee ka madhva pilaikay*
> *Matvali kar leeni ray mosay naina milaikay*

Abida Parveen singing Amir Khurso, and that too live, and suddenly I start laughing. I laugh until there is no laughter left to hear, and all I hear is the sound of life coming full circle. I look up and see Faiz standing a few feet away eating milky white chum chum draped in leaves of silver, better known as *chandi kay warq*.

'Hello again,' he says.

I smile and say, 'I thought you loved shahi tukray?'

'I do, but tonight I'm in the mood for the sweetness of white and the sound of silver.'

> *A fleeting glance we sometimes get,*
> *We've been with someone we've never met,*
> *We've known them before we are unaware,*
> *Affairs of the heart, we may have shared.*

ROGHAN JOSH

I've had roghan josh once in my life; I vividly remember the unforgettable aroma and deliciously tender melt-in-your-mouth texture of the meat.

Roghan josh has the honour of being one of the seven permanent dishes in the thirty-six-course wazwan. Wazwan is a ceremonial and traditional Kashmiri feast and was introduced to the region in the fourteenth century with the arrival of Taimur Lung. History tells us the tale of a large migration of skilled artists and cooks to Kashmir from Samarkand.

The use of heeng or asafoetida and its unique flavour and aroma in the making of Kashmiri roghan josh is essential, as is the use of the fiery Kashmiri red chilli and the aromatic Kashmiri garam masala, which is different from the popularly used Punjabi garam masala.

Ingredients

2 lb goat meat (preferably leg meat, cut in small pieces)
½ cup oil
2 to 3 bay leaves
2 cinnamon sticks
2 to 3 sabut lal mirch (whole dried red pepper)
½ tsp level heeng
Salt to taste
12 to 16 oz yogurt
1 ½ to 2 tsp Kashmiri or deghi chilli powder
1 to 1½ tsp level ginger powder
1 to 1 ½ tsp coriander powder
8 to 12 green cardamom pods
½ to 1 tsp Kashmiri garam masala
2 cups of water

Method

Heat oil and fry bay leaves, cinnamon sticks and sabut lal mirch for a minute, adding meat. Stir, adding salt and asafoetida. Stir until meat releases water and it dries, add a little water stirring constantly. Add yogurt and red chilli powder, stirring constantly until meat is half done (20 to 25 minutes), adding a little water as needed; then add ginger powder and coriander powder. Cook until meat is completely tender (adding a little water if required), sprinkle freshly ground Kashmiri garam masala and cardamom, stir, and initiate sealed pot cooking for 10 minutes.

Your deliciously aromatic roghan josh is ready to be served.

◆

SHAHI TUKRAY

What is it about shahi tukray that we love so much? Like biryani, this *baadshahi* dessert can also be traced to the Mughlai kitchens. However, it remains a mystery as to how this twist on bread pudding came to the subcontinent. Did Babur's entourage bring it with them in the sixteenth century when travelling to India, as most believe? Or did the British East India Company eat it in the form of bread pudding which later evolved into shahi tukray, the delectable Mughlai meetha seeped in the royal aromas of cardamom and saffron, sweetness of sugar and nuts, and the smooth texture of full-cream milk and heavy cream.

Bread is a staple that goes back millennia, and it is commonly believed that chefs in the old days, as now, disliked throwing away leftover bread and, therefore, created innovative recipes, both sweet and savoury. Leftover bread was used to thicken broth and sweet pudding, used as croutons in soups, stuffing and coating as bread crumbs; it could be baked, fried or stove-cooked, or used as an edible bread bowl. During the middle ages a hollowed loaf, now referred to as the bread bowl, was commonly used to drink hot or cold sweet milk, puddings, broth, eggs; and this is how the bread pudding came to be. A rustic utensil stumbles upon the simple sweet goodness of milk, eggs and bread and the world has its bread pudding with many twists.

Shahi tukray, literally means royal pieces—'shahi' meaning fan or follower of the royals in Persian, and 'tukray', a Hindi word meaning pieces, bites, or scraps. So why did the royal chefs decide to do away with eggs in this Mughlai dessert? My guess is that they wanted a textured softness in the bite instead of the fluffiness of eggs; therefore, the uncrusted bread was first fried in ghee, or butter and then baked in sweetened creamy milk flavoured with saffron, cardamom and rosewater and garnished with almonds, pistachios and raisins, and finally decorated with chandi or sonay kay warq. Legend also suggests that initially a little bit of khoya, milk thickened by heating (currently referred to as condensed milk), was used in the making of shahi tukray.

It is popularly believed that shahi tukray was a favourite of the Mughal Emperors to break fast with in the month of Ramazan, and thus the practice continues even today making it a very desirable dish on the Iftar menu, and famously served at the festive occasions of Eid-ul-Fitr and Eid-ul-Azha.

It is believed that the imperial Mughal kitchen was home to generations of chefs who were connoisseurs of world cuisines and developed dishes that were influenced by Persian, Turkic and Central Asian foods reflecting north Indian cooking, distinctly from Delhi, Uttar Pradesh, Lahore, Hyderabad (the Indian city) and from Bangladesh.

Ingredients

12 slices of white bread (uncrusted)
1¼ cups oil
23 oz whole milk
6 oz sugar
1 to 2 tsp yellow food colouring
½ tsp cardamom seeds
4 oz of condensed milk
15 to 20 blanched almonds cut lengthwise in slivers
Chandi kay warq

Method

Heat oil and deep fry uncrusted bread until light golden brown, put in sieve to drain oil, pouring drained oil back in the pan. Double stack bread in a baking dish, and in a separate bowl mix sugar with cold milk, adding food colouring to your preference. Sprinkle cardamom seeds on fried bread, pour milk and sugar mixture and bake in a pre-heated 400 degrees oven for 20 to 25 minutes.

Take out from oven, sprinkle blanched almonds, pour condensed milk and bake in oven again for 8 to 10 minutes. Cool and serve, warm or cold.

◆

CHANAY KE DAAL KA HALWA

Chanay ke daal ka halwa is my absolute favourite dessert. I fell in love with it some decades ago when my little self used to stand in the corner of our home terrace, devouring a plate of chanay ke daal ka halwa, unaware of the peeping auntie from the house next door. Yes, I was a fat, chubby if one wants to be kind, little kid always ready to sneak chanay ke daal or gajar ka halwa. I remember my anticipation and excitement on noticing that Ammi was getting ready for siesta, and Jalal our telltale cook had closed his kitchen too. That translated into me gliding to the freezer, stealing a small frozen portion of halwa and heating it to edible perfection in the January of Karachi.

Yes, it was the early eighties and I was a pre-teen. This was my afternoon romance with halwa, and it lasted for just a season, and the reason? Naushad Auntie's Chinese whispers to Ammi.

Halwa finds its roots in the Arabic language and refers to many dense or compact desserts. Originally, halwa was either flour-based or used various nuts with sugar, milk and butter to create a sweet gelatinous, or hardened nutty dessert. It is commonly believed that this kind of halwa was introduced to the settlers in India through trade with the Middle East and Asia Minor during the expansion of the Mughal Empire.

The shared food heritage between Pakistan and India is fascinating; we share the same food stories and love the same foods, and can rightfully lay claim to most foods as our own. This not only makes for a delightfully interesting dinner conversation with friends, but also a common ground to share family recipes and stories. My mom made scrumptious chanay ke daal ka halwa, the kind that made a petty thief out of me, and here it is, from my kitchen to yours.

Ingredients

2 cups chanay ke daal
Milk
Sugar
Oil
15 green cardamoms
½ cup blanched almonds, chopped
¼ cup pistachios

Method

Soak daal for 6 to 8 hours. Drain and grind in a food processor until fine. Pour the ground daal into a heavy based pan, adding milk, stirring periodically, once the milk starts evaporating, add oil, cardamom and sugar to taste. Now begins the heavy stirring, keep stirring and adding oil until the consistency is right. As you keep stirring, the colour of the halwa starts changing to a golden brown. Do not lose heart, keep stirring, adding oil if required, and slowly but gradually the oil will separate. Keep stirring until oil separates and the colour is a rich beautiful golden. Garnish with nuts and serve.

◆

LASSI

Lassi, rustic and refreshingly delicious to the core, is believed to have originated centuries ago in the region of Punjab where milk, like the chappati, has almost always been a staple. During the intense Indian summer of the Punjab, the hardworking farmers used to consume a chilled concoction of milk, curd and sugar. The drink was served in clay pots, and at times chilled in the cool rivers flowing through the villages. The sweet and tangy drink gained popularity all over the subcontinent and it came to be noticed that its consumption during the summer months kept the body hydrated and refreshingly cool. Lassi became a favourite of the region and today ingredients like mint, ginger, mango, cumin and cilantro are added to the drink, but there is no better lassi than the original—a happy blend of yogurt, milk, chilled river water and a lot of sugar.

Ingredients (2 to 4 glasses)

8 oz yogurt
4 oz milk
4 oz cold water
Ice cubes as needed
Sugar as needed.

Method

Put together in a blender and blend until froth forms, pour into glasses and enjoy.

Chapter 5

Mazaars

Dama Dum Mast Qalander

Monsoon 1995

I've never said *fateha* at the graveside of Hazrat Daata Ganj Baksh, and what better time to pay my respects than the present. As my four partners in crime pack their bags and head to Karachi, I decide to stay on an extra day and head to the green-domed shrine of the great Sufi saint.

Rehana Tai is eager to accompany me, but I want this to be a solitary expedition and am successful in convincing her to let the driver and his wife accompany me.

Sameera, the driver's wife, and I are dropped a ten-minute walk away from the shrine. It's seven in the evening and time for sunset Magrib Prayers, and expectedly there is din, noise, cars, pollution, and great rush. Everyone seems to be in a hurry to get somewhere, but where that somewhere is, nobody knows. I see traffic and bodies passing me by, but my mind is in a whirl and I notice nothing specific. I pick up my pace and a panting Sameera frantically tries to match my step and breathlessly says, 'Walk slow, Baji.'

'Oh, sorry,' I say, not slowing my pace or my heart rate.

I pass the main white passage, entering the alleyway leading to the large courtyard facing the mausoleum that houses the grave of Daata Sahib. I slip off my sandals and hug them to my chest proceeding through the large quadrangle and stand outside the doors, say a quick prayer, and then walk to the far corner by the entrance and sit on the cool marble floor.

Waiting.

There is excitement, my eyes search the crowd, and suddenly I get a feeling of déjà vu.

Who am I searching for? It's all too familiar, the *qawaali*, the smell of the earth after the rain, the yearning, the raindrops, the open courtyard, standing alone at the altar, the shrine, the *dhamaal*, the song, the panic.

The *qawaals* begin their rendition of Amir Khusro's devotional poetry 'Mun Kunto Maula' as the sema builds to a crescendo. Frenzied devotees take to the floor, swirling, spinning and dancing to the lyrics, impassioned.

Why am I here?

What am I waiting for?

Who am I waiting for?

And I run out of the courtyard, pulling Sameera with me.

∾

Monsoon, Delhi 1945

Shireen stood outside the shrine of Nizamuddin Auliya holding Sharmeena's hand. The girls were wearing veil and burka and were eagerly waiting for Sharmeena's older brother to escort them to the abode of the *nikaahkawan*. The best friends were excited on becoming sisters-in-law today. They had been waiting for an hour by the graveside of Ziauddin Barani who lay within the plaza of the shrine. Shireen let her fingers slip from Sharmeena's hand and walked to the tomb of Amir Khusro some feet away, blessing him for his devotional qawaali.

Amir Khusro devoted his life to his mentor, he loved Nizamuddin Auliya, and the allegiance inspired a spiritual celebration of timeless poetry. The tabla and the accompanying qawaali was building intensity, much like Shireen. She hugged her slippers to her chest, biting her lip and mouthing the lyrics of the tenderly romantic 'Rung' by the transcendent Khusro. Her anticipation to experience the physicality of the euphoric poetry made her smile. She was finally going to wed the man she loved.

He said he would meet her at the graveside of his ancestor Ziauddin Barani. Shireen walked back to Barani's graveside and said a prayer for him. She sat down, leaning on the wooden pillar by the grave and wondered at the coincidence of Ziauddin Barani's grave being in close proximity to that of Amir Khusro. They were believed to be companions and ate together often, and Barani was said to be a connoisseur of Khusro poetry, describing his poet mystic friend as 'incomparable'. Maybe when Khusro first wrote 'Rung' he read the lyrics to his friend and like the entire Hindustan, made a fan out of him too.

Suddenly, Shireen felt hungry and the smell of sweet yellow rice, zarda, enticed her. She turned to Sharmeena and said, 'Let's go eat, it's lunchtime and surely langar distribution outside the shrine must have zarda, pulao and biryani on its menu. Let's get in line for langar before the Zuhr call for prayer, otherwise the lines are going to get very long.'

Shireen ran out with Sharmeena on her tail. She could not curtail her excitement, and in celebration of her pending nuptials, decided to load up on sweet honeyed zarda, sprinkled with khoya, raisins and almonds. She dug her right hand into the plate and made a morsel, and hungrily took her first bite, marinating in its sugary sweetness. The sweetness calmed her anxiety and she sat and savoured the moment, wondering how she would get her hands on zarda, such as this, across the seven seas.

'What if Bhaiya comes and we are not at our meeting point inside the courtyard of Barani's graveside?' asked Sharmeena, exasperated at the overzealousness of her soon to be sister-in-law.

At a distance, Shireen heard the faint ringing of the chimes. It was the Northbrook Clock Tower, the famed ghantaghar, standing tall in Chandni Chowk. She recalled her father telling her about the massacre of 1919 when several Indians were gunned down under the clock tower by British soldiers for demanding freedom from the British Raj. She listened for the clock to strike one—reminiscent of the church bells at her school in Simla; she loved the sound of bells. They reminded her of happy days at boarding school and wondered what the Big Ben sounded like to Londoners.

'He said to wait for him inside the courtyard from midday to 1 p.m., and if he doesn't come between those hours, he'd come at 4 p.m.,' replied Shireen. There was spunk in her gait and sparkle in her eyes as she got in line to get a second helping of zarda. Her insides yearned for more and she greedily looked at the feast being distributed amongst the poor and the hungry, and wondered why all the mazaars of Sufi saints were a haven for distribution of free food.

A sea of humanity sat eating langar: homeless urchins grabbing on to plates of free food, children hungrily chowing on rice and korma, desperate mothers demanding plates of meals to take home to their hungry children, old men and women enjoying a delicious hot meal, and in their wake the likes of Shireen and Sharmeena.

Shireen sat down on the footpath by the shrine and absorbed the mayhem. She pondered the knowledge that the Auliya was famed for distributing langar and his magnanimous spirit and open kitchen served free meals to all who came with an empty stomach, or with a broken spirit. His largeness of spirit, scholarly ways, complete devotion to his Maker, and to imparting spiritual guidance to his devotees, made him an inspirational giant through the ages and his reputation lives on to this day.

Sharmeena was getting anxious, when was her brother going to come? The clouds looked ominous, and there was still the nikaah to be solemnized and Shireen's departure with her brother across the seven seas. She squeezed Shireen's hand and said, 'Let's go to Humayun's *makbara*, its right around the corner. I promise we'll be back soon.'

Shireen had never gone inside and was awestruck by the artistry of the monument. She stood centre-stage in the *charbagh*, the Quranic inspired paradise-like gardens flanking the red sandstone structure housing the tomb of the Mughal Emperor. The water fountains remained silent, but promised a magnificent show of water and light on a moonlit night.

She wondered how the makers of grandiose buildings such as the magnificent Taj Mahal and the Shish Mahal had perished without leaving a trace, leaving only buildings behind and no legacy in the form of a bloodline. So much for being a royal, it was only as grand as long as it lasted, she thought. She pondered the acumen of the architects, engineers and mechanics of yesteryears and applauded their integral genius as the splendid innovators in the rise of the Mughal Empire. But tragically the magnificent palaces, mosques, gardens or fortresses could not save the grand dynasty.

Why? The answer was pathetically simple; for just as the empire peaked, its zenith courted by arrogance, it slowly but surely began to crumble and fall, coerced by weakness, intrigue, greed and corruption, much like the king sitting atop his house of cards.

And today the surviving descendants of the Mughals were lost in translation and time. She felt a little smug as she thought about her ancestors and the legacy they had passed on in the form of their bloodline, and of course the legendary pulao.

She regretted that she had never visited the Taj Mahal in Agra, or the Shah Jahan Mosque in Thatta. Her father had travelled to the city of Thatta a few years ago and had asked her to join him, but she never had and was overwhelmed by disappointment over that. She loved visiting places of worship—churches, temples, mosques or gurdwaras. She laughed off the feeling of disappointment that lingered, and voiced her thoughts to Sharmeena. 'Maybe you can go there in another life, or maybe this one,' said her friend, as she shrugged her shoulders.

The girls decided to head back to Ziauddin Barani's graveside hand-in-hand. Shireen's mind was elsewhere and she did not notice the cycle collision, the dog barking menacingly at the children throwing stones at it, or the madman looking at her and repeating, 'He's not coming, no, he's not.'

She kept walking, and then she waited, until day turned to night, and night turned to shame, and shame turned to choice, and choice turned to sorrow, and sorrow turned to gluttony.

≈

The Alsatian puppy is following a pattern of play, it licks my hand and just as quickly turns its attention to the hot pink duster on the floor, repeating the sequence every twenty seconds. It has been doing so for the past five minutes. Sofia sweeps it off the floor, it squirms and yelps in her hands and jumps to the floor finding its way back to me.

'He keeps finding his way back to you, shuttling between you and the hot pink duster, almost like Faiz at the haveli,' whispers a very amused Sofia.

I glare at her tossing the pink duster and retort, 'Here, you keep the duster, I'll keep the puppy.' Both of us are sitting on the verandah footsteps playing with Abbu's latest import. I want to name him Simba, but Abbu is insistent on calling him Leo. So Leo it is.

Out comes Jalal with two chilled glasses of cold coffee and the handset of the cordless phone. 'Ayesha baby, Ajit Samra is on the phone for you.' Ajit and I not only kept in touch after our lower Sindh jaunt some years ago, but the three of us—him, me and Sofia—became the best of friends, and he has offered to conduct a photo-shoot for our greeting card series titled, 'Life's A Beach'.

We are deciding on a Karachi beach location where Ajit will capture simple and timeless beach shots, Sofia will caption a sentiment, an emotion, a feeling in context to the photograph and I will finish it with artwork, making it into a saleable finished product. We are hoping to wrap this project soon and are looking to schedule a day for the photo shoot in the upcoming weeks. And since the monsoon season is behind us, and the beach tides are safer, we are planning to make a day and night getaway of the entire project, and making a picnic out of it.

Sofia takes a sip of the cold coffee, signalling a thumbs-up to Jalal and in the process grabs the cordless phone from his hand. She animatedly discusses the photo shoot and some of the catch phrases and captions she has in mind for the series, while I savour the taste of the cold coffee and ponder our joyously memorable exchange with Ajit at Fahmeeda Soomro's house some years ago. I wistfully reminisce about that fabulous and educational afternoon in Thatta when Ajit Samra not only became our friend, but much more to our wonderful hosts, Janoo and Fahmeeda Soomro. There was food, best friends, and the whole world to talk about, and it was certainly turning out to be my kind of an afternoon.

That afternoon, Fahmeeda Soomro told us tales of the journey of the Palla fish and its cultural significance to the people of Sindh. I was mesmerized by her fables of the Indus. 'The Indus is an ancient river, and so is the province of Sindh—home to the Palla fish, Lal Shahbaz Qalander, Zinda Pir, Jhulay Lal, Mohenjo-Daro, poetry and love. My family has lived in Sindh for centuries,' she said. 'They kept moving around from city to city, but have not left the region for hundreds of years. This fish you eat,' she said, pointing towards our plates, 'is the sweet-water Palla, which is intrinsically oilier in texture than the salt-water Palla. Their flavours are mildly different, but both are delicious.

'Legend suggests,' she continued, 'that as the fish swims upstream in the Indus it absorbs flavour, and once it passes the shrine of Khizar, the saint who lives forever, it gathers blessings which transform it into silver and give it exceptional taste. The everlasting saint, Zinda Khizar gifts the now silvery fish a red dot on the forehead, the bindi.'

Pointing to a picture on the wall she said, 'The region of Sindh, and Hindustan, both find their roots in the flow of this great river Indus. And as for the Palla, it has spiritual and cultural significance for the entire region. It belongs to the Sindhis much like the River Indus belongs to this land. You see that painting on the wall with the saint sitting on a silver fish? That is Jhulay Lal, sitting on the Palla fish. He is considered secular in nature, much like Shahbaz Qalander. It's wonderful how food and Sufism bring people together.'

'Fahmeeda ji, you are so right,' Ajit had responded, 'My last name is Samra, Ajit Samra. My family has lived in Punjab for centuries, but I trace my roots to the region surrounding the upper Indus belt. Up until the fourteenth century my family lived in Sindh, but with the spread of Islam through the Islamic missionary work of Pir Jalaluddin Bukhari, some Samras converted to Islam and became Soomros. Many remained Hindu, while some converted to Sikhism much later. I belong to the Samra Jatt tribe, but I can guarantee that your husband, Lateef Soomro ji, and my family must be related some twenty-five generations ago. Our forefathers must have been brothers in the fourteenth century.'

At that Janoo had jumped up off the floor, flamboyantly hugged Samra and said, 'Oh my Bhai, where were you, we have been looking for you for over five hundred years,' and the room had erupted in laughter. The twin boys high-fived, the seventeen-year-old girls danced, as did Sofia and I. On cue, the entire group broke into a rendition of the Sufi qawaali, 'Dama Dum Mast Qalandar', and somewhere in the back of my head I heard another song:

> Our hands clapped in music
> Our voices sung in sync
> Our bodies danced in utopian glee
> Let the tale of the Indus begin

❧

Abbu is an odd combination of savvy and simple, and his simple side, and a strong influence of Tayajee Tyyab, convinced him to start following a quintessential Pir Sahib some years ago. The kind with the long silk robe and comically extravagant gestures we read about in books, or watch on the screen, the kind that seeks remuneration in cash and kind from the simpleton in exchange for playing interpreter between the simpleton and his Maker. Oddly enough that's the kind of Pir that Abbu is currently awed by.

We have been hoping for a while that this phase will pass since hope springs eternal, and I see signs of that happening since Pir

Sahib has been asking for monies, and too often. While Abbu's devotion seems to be waning, Pir Sahib's devotional squad seems to be growing every day. People who join his list of followers seem mostly to be from the educated middle class. Sounds rather odd, but it is not as rare an occurrence as we would like to believe.

Most people follow some kind of Pir. They maybe impressed by someone, inspired by someone, in love with someone, obsessed with someone, in bonded labour to someone, scared of someone, be a spiritual devotee of someone, or a chamcha to someone (akin to the satellite attendant in Greek plays). Essentially proving it is easier to follow someone else's lead, rather than following your own.

Dadi is rather practical about the Pir and disciple pairing. 'Life is simple and we are aware of that as children, but taught behaviour, learnt experiences, choices, and emotional baggage make life difficult for us and for those around us,' she says. 'Once life unfolds as complicated, we need a middleman, an executor of sorts to keep reminding us that the outcome of our choices will become easier, however true or false that claim maybe, and that is what a pseudo Pir does: he gives us false hope.

'In essence,' she notes sagely, 'difficult life episodes—unless pre-ordained—only improve once our choices improve. An honest mentor, spiritual guide, or teacher mostly teaches life's principles to his apprentice or student. He insists that practice of skill and improved thought, discipline and commitment improves life and nothing else, and self-reflection and introspection help elevate personal spirituality and humility.

'The practical form of this is prayer and meditation,' she concludes, 'the very essence of organized religion. It teaches discipline, mind control and self-control, honing refinement of spirit. Your father will move away from Pir Sahib soon. He is a sensible man.'

I think her prediction is going to soon come true.

Pir Sahib's extravagant ways are comical. And since I am in the mood to confess, I have attended many a *mehfil-e-sema* and talk from experience. The choice to attend the *mehfilain* as a young teen was an easy one, since there was free food at the gatherings.

We would walk into an audience, the size of which depended on the day of the week. It was usually large on Thursdays, the start of the weekend with Friday being a public holiday. Initially, Pir Sahib appeared fair and balanced, listening to the woes of all and offering seemingly sage counsel, but that somehow changed over the years. As his popularity grew, his morality dipped; sadly, such are the ways of power.

The congregation room that Abbu visited was ostentatious, dressed in ornately carved golden sofas upholstered in emerald green printed fabric, and overly incensed with a sweet pungent smell. The central dangling light fixture was a cheap knockoff of an original Murano glass chandelier, emanating the brightness of the midday sun. The red carpet on the floor was thick and plush, and definitely made sitting on the floor less of an ache, while the edges were lined with soft large cushions. Large calligraphic wall-hangings beckoned at eye level, and viewing the devotees from the low daybed, referred to as the 'masnut', was Pir Sahib Hashmat Hakeem Sheikhanni, cunning, judging and swindling.

I would walk into an audience of people from all income groups, skin tones and ethnicities, discussing their burdens. It appeared the more they talked the lighter their distresses became. I somehow always found the perfect spot behind Pir Sahib's special council, and was privy to the baggage people were unloading. Some stories were pathetic to hear, others not so much.

Attending the mehfil somehow became story time and was the perfect Thursday night in town. I would listen to stories and eat biryani, much like Ya Bhai's great aunt Haleema Bai in her days at her grandfather's house at the Bombay gatherings. I vividly remember Ya Bhai telling me that his great aunt used to insist, 'stories and food remain the same, only faces change, and those too only vaguely. The same faces keep coming back every few generations to eat the same food and live out the same stories.'

The concept is fascinating to me and implies that we as humans are living in a relay race, passing the baton of our choices on to the next generation, transferring our burdens and blessings to them. I sat in the back hearing all kinds of stories and wondered if families are like a photo-mosaic—going through generations, with each generation devoting one small photograph to the entire montage, with the final artwork being displayed on the day of reckoning.

Does that mean our decisions have long-term inter-generational consequences and impact our future generations?

Probably.

Consequently our decisions can never be independent or absolutely final, and if by chance we manage to finish a storyline then fate and our choices combine and coax us towards new beginnings, the beginnings we leave behind as building blocks for our children. We inherit baggage and favours from the past, do away with some of it, adding our own and passing it on to our children.

Are we just a link from the past into the future, and nothing else?

Maybe.

I vividly remember a man sitting at Pir Sahib's feet, desperately wanting to escape his past by breaking the cycle of misfortune he inherited from his father. Mercenary Pir Sahib shared no wisdom with him. However, I remember the cook serving the food advising the pathetic man, 'Mend your ways, be a better man, make honourable choices if you want to leave a better legacy for your children in comparison to the one you inherited.'

However, my focus that day was only the dasterkhwan, a lavish spread of biryani, zarda, korma and haleem beckoning me as miserable stories unfolded. I sat focused on the food, oblivious to the reality that I was a part of a photo-mosaic too, a photo-mosaic that was still out of focus, but surely beginning to gain clarity with progressing time.

∾

I ran to open the gate, the bell rang twice but all the domestic staff seemed to have disappeared, as had my brothers. I ran through the verandah, almost tripped on the rug and landed two steps down on the front porch. I called out to Jalal and the gate guard, but to no avail. Swearing under my breath, I opened the gate to a smiling Imran.

'Hi, I came to drop these papers for Yahya. He said he'd pick them up from here. How are you? Haven't heard from you in a while. I thought you wanted to do the Punjab food tour?' he said, handing a large yellow manila envelope to me.

'Hi, and thanks,' I said, 'I'll pass this on to Ya Bhai, he'll drop in sometime later in the evening, and I plan to take the Punjab food tour in the winter, during the orange harvest season, I believe the orange groves in Toba Tek Singh are glorious. I'm going to sign up for the December trip. Actually, why don't you sign me up, I'll round up my four usual suspects.'

'Hi Ayesha,' said a voice from inside Imran's car.

'Hi,' I replied, flushed, blushed, and a little breathless.

'It's been a while, how are you?' asked Faiz, as he bent his head to get a better look at me.

I heard a flustered voice in my head give a speech on how I was, but nothing came out.

I wanted to say how I had thought about this moment a hundred times.

How I wanted to be wearing something else.

How I wanted to be wearing a little more Samsara.

How I wanted to linger a little longer to answer the question.

How I had stayed up entire nights thinking about him and then fallen asleep with thoughts of him.

How I wanted to ask him a million questions.

How ecstatic I felt hearing his voice.

How euphoric it felt seeing him.

How I wanted this moment to last a little longer.

But all that came out was, 'I'm well Faiz, how have you been, how's the hydropower project going?'

Faiz stepped out of the Civic, resting one arm on the open door and the other on the roof of the car and replied, 'It's going. These government things are real slow. Too much red tape, approvals needed from countless different places, but it's moving at a steady pace. Did you start your greeting card venture? I think it's a great niche and one that needs to be tapped.'

Just then Yahya's Pajero pulled up and Imran walked towards it. The two men enthusiastically exchanged greetings, acknowledged us fleetingly, and still talking casually walked onto the verandah inside, leaving Faiz and I standing outside the gates of the house.

'You want to come in? Ya Bhai's not invited us to join him, but gone in uninvited himself,' I said laughing nervously.

As we walked onto the verandah, I politely asked Faiz to take a seat and sat diagonal to him telling tales of the sofa, and elaborating on the pathetic plight of the furniture-maker, the grandson, a few generations removed of the Mughal Emperor Babur, or for that matter a descendant of Taimur Lung.

Faiz listened, observed my nervously animated gestures and passionate rendering, as I lost in my excited world jumped from one topic to another hoping to unwittingly pull him in, one gesture at a time. I heard a voice in the back of my head telling me to tone down the flamboyance, but my mind got busy with advice from the heart. Prudent of the mind to pay attention, for unlike the game of evolved scheme and method, falling in love is a game where the frenzy of the feeling heart leads the thoughtful mind.

Suddenly, Ya Bhai's voice broke in, 'Have you selected a location for the 'Life's A Beach' photo shoot? Paradise Point, Hawke's bay, Sandspit, French Beach, or Cape Monze? Do let me know so I can make arrangements for an overnight stay.'

'I will,' I replied, thankful to be saved from myself. 'Will you be bringing a truckload of biryani for the bonfire night?' I asked.

'We can do without your sarcasm. No biryani for you, ever! Try asking for biryani on the house now, all you'll get is boiled eggs, and maybe barbecue from down the street,' replied Yahya laughing, referring to the world famous barbeque restaurant, Bundoo Khan, located a mile down the road from B. Bees.

'No one can stop me from having biryani at B. Bees, ever,' I declared as Jalal walked in pushing a trolley with evening chai, accompanied by delicious delights.

The trolley was decked more than usual. There was a platter of vegetable pakoray and samosay, mixed alloo chaat, kabab, dahi baray, cucumber sandwiches, plain cake, naan khatai and hubshi halwa.

'Is this the usual evening trolley at your house? My God, you beat the trolley at my house. I thought the evening tea-trolley was only a big deal with my mom,' said Faiz, amused at the extravagant spread.

The romance of chai and the subcontinent go way back. The

English may have invented teatime, but the desis of the world embraced it with such warmth that it's now become synonymous with the subcontinent. Among other things, best friends are made over a cup of chai and many a match made in heaven is solidified or impaired over a cup of chai too. Much like the one that I unknowingly damaged a few months ago, or the one I am, unwittingly, busy solidifying currently.

'I was designing cards to celebrate teatime, and decided to do some research on the spread of tea in Pakistan and India,' I said. My audience looked genuinely interested, so I held nothing back. 'Do you know that the spread of tea is believed to be one of the first significant product promotion success stories of the nineteenth century in the subcontinent? Gora saab realized the niche and estimated the future population of South Asia, and maybe tapped onto our penchant for all things good.'

Since the audience was still hooked, I continued. 'He slowly seduced villages, cities, neighbourhoods, railway stations, army barracks and factories with free cups of chai in the evening, and once the desis fell in love and became addicts, gora saab detached the free cups of chai, put a price on them and started selling chai to us in teabags and boxes. And thus began our love affair with *shaam ki chai*.' I patted myself on the back for having recently read the article 'Teatime in the Subcontinent'.

Faiz bent across the table as I handed him his cup of chai and was fleetingly greeted by tones of warm sandalwood and masculine cedar, refreshed with a citrus scent. I made a mental note to go to Agha's and smell all the men's cologne, until I narrowed it down to the fragrance that Faiz was wearing.

'Do you want some naan khatai?' I asked. 'It's the best in the West.'

'Best in the West! Last I checked, Karachi sits on the southernmost tip of Pakistan,' said an amused Faiz, getting ready to volley the answer that was about to come his way.

'Oh, I know, I just said West because it rhymes with best,' I said laughing, and then quietened some to let the others make conversation. As I settled in my rocking chair with a cup of tea, Faiz's back was to me and I noticed the way his hair fell above his shirt collar, the movement of his right shoulder as he leaned forward to set down his empty cup of tea, his left arm resting on the armrest, lean and tanned with the shirt-sleeve rolled to the elbow. There he sat wearing a textured blue cotton shirt, the colour of a cloudless midday sky, trendy jeans and camel coloured suede boots with spurs, oblivious to my deepening interest.

I finished my cup of chai and picked up a second naan khatai to soothe my nerves. I almost took a bite and then heard Sofia's voice in my mind telling me not to, and instead crumbled the desi biscuit into the teacup making it soggy and unpalatable. If nothing else that would prevent me from eating it, I thought.

'What did the naan khatai do? What are you punishing it for?' inquired a voice from across the room. I half smiled at Faiz who had turned his chair in my direction, and said, 'I love biscuits, can never stop at eating one. So I either devour the second or destroy it.'

'Why not just eat it?'

'Well, because biscuits and me have a story, a sweet delicious love story. We all have our vices, mine are biscuits, desi or otherwise.'

Faiz looked at me intently as I spoke, and then smiling softly said, 'Maybe it's time to break away from biscuits and start another love story.'

'Maybe it is,' I replied pensively.

～

SINDHI BIRYANI AT MAZAARS

The energy was electric, the dhamaal at its peak, the qawaali being rendered by none other than Ghulam Fareed Sabri, '*Bhar day jholee mayree ya Mohammed*,' and the langar at the blue-tiled Sufi shrine of Lal Shahbaz Qalandar was serving Sindhi biryani. The year was 1981, and there I was, a ten-year-old mesmerized by the tempo and volume of the beating drums in sync with my beating heart. I soaked in the atmosphere, the music, the frenzy of the *mureeds*, and, of course, the fiery Sindhi biryani; delicious, rich, exotic, a perfect manifestation of its surroundings.

Biryani is a celebratory dish in more ways than one, it is cooked at the time of celebration and when it is cooked it is time to celebrate. It is the Mughlai twist to the pulao. Whereas the variety of pulao dishes are known for their aroma, different kinds of biryani platters are known for their spices, masala and unique fiery flavours. Having lived in Karachi all my life, I know the taste of a deliciously spicy Sindhi biryani. The masala-steeped potatoes, the tangy alloo bukhara (dried plums/prunes), mint and khatta dahi (sour yogurt) render the Sindhi biryani masala different in taste; a masala spicier than that of most regional biryanis, and the proportion of the masala to the rice is a little more than for most biryanis.

The yogurt used in most biryanis is sweet, but the Sindhi biryani requires it to be khatta. Red and green chillies, and whole garam masala are used vigorously. The cooking style is somewhat different from other regional biryanis too, and there is no use of rose or kewra water, as is common in most Mughlai dishes.

Ingredients
For the masala
3 lb mutton (leg meat)

3 mugs basmati rice
5 medium potatoes, cut in half
8 oz to 12 oz oil
2 large onions, sliced
4 tsp freshly chopped garlic
5 to 6 medium sized tomatoes
12 to 14 prunes
Salt to taste
3 to 4 tsp red chilli powder
2 teaspoons cumin seeds
Whole garam masala (12 to 14 cloves, 12 to 14 peppercorns, 2 cinnamon sticks, 5 black cardamom pods, 10 green cardamom pods)
4 to 6 bay leaves
6 oz to 8 oz sour yogurt
6 to 8 green chillies
½ bunch coriander leaves
10 to 12 mint leaves
Orange food colour (a pinch)
8 oz to 16 oz water

Ingredients to be added to boiling rice
Salt to taste
4 bay leaves
Whole garam masala (4 cinnamon sticks, 3 black cardamom pods, ¼ tsp black peppercorns, ¼ tsp cloves)

Method
For the masala
Heat oil and fry sliced onions until golden brown and set aside 2 to 3 tbsp to be used later as garnish.

To the remaining oil and onions, add the chopped ginger and

garlic, tomatoes, prunes, salt, red chilli powder, bay leaves, cumin and whole garam masala.

Fry for 5 to 10 minutes on high heat, stirring constantly, adding yogurt, meat and water as required. Once meat is three-fourths done add peeled potatoes. Cook for 14 to 20 minutes or until meat and potatoes are tender, adding the greens and stirring on high heat. The biryani masala is ready. Set it aside.

For the rice

In a separate pot boil water, adding whole garam masala (4 cinnamon sticks, 3 black cardamom pods, ¼ tsp black peppercorns, ¼ tsp cloves) and bay leaves. Once water comes to a boil add pre-soaked rice, cooking it till tender crisp, since we cook the rice completely in the dum phase.

Drain, layer the pot with rice, top with a layer of biryani masala, adding a second layer of rice. Top with fried onions, sprinkle food colouring, sliced tomatoes, cilantro, mint and green chillies. Seal pot with foil and lid. Cook at full heat for 5 minutes, and medium to low heat for 15 minutes, to complete the dum. Let sit for 10 minutes, mix and serve.

◆

ZARDA

Zarda, pure joy and simple goodness, much like Mother and Marie Biscuits. Yes, zarda happens to be the simplest of desserts defining the best of joys; hence it is a sweet delight served at weddings, Shab-e-Baraat, Raksha Bandhan, and many other celebratory occasions popular in the subcontinent. For me, zarda never held much appeal, until maturity set in and I started appreciating the subtle sweetness of diluted sugar playing magic with the simplicity of basmati rice, the royal fragrance of cardamom, and golden hue of our life force, the sun.

Indeed, the development of Mughlai cuisine was sustained by the availability of a wide variety of new and imported ingredients, which made it all the more delectable. By synthesizing different cuisines from Hindustan, Arabia, Persia, Central Asia and Europe, and importing raw ingredients, the Mughals gave the region a sweet rice delight like zarda and the sweet and savoury mutanjan.

Many of the modern subcontinental foods have evolved to their current form, and are greatly influenced, cooked and styled after the cuisine prepared in the royal kitchens of the Mughals. It is well established that Akbar, grandson of Babur, participated greatly in the happenings of the royal kitchen. He enforced stringent rules of kitchen etiquette that the staff adhered to without exception.

Food historians believe that rice travelled to Europe from the subcontinent. Hence we can safely believe that sweet rice in its basic form is an ancient dish, enjoyed and savoured by young and old. The yellow zarda is a favoured dessert distributed at Sufi shrines that dot the subcontinent. I have enjoyed eating it at Baba Abdullah Shah Ghazi's Shrine, Lal Shahbaz Qalandar's Shrine and at Mongo Pir, and since I was never a big fan of the zarda, I always mixed it up with savoury biryani or pulao to make a mutanjan of sorts.

Ingredients

2 cups basmati rice
4 oz butter
1 cup and 1 tbsp sugar
¼ to ⅓ cup blanched and halved almonds
¼ cup raisins
Pistachio (optional; I prefer not to add them)
2 to 3 tbsp freshly squeezed orange juice
½ to 1 tsp orange zest

4 to 6 green cardamom pods
2 to 3 strands saffron (optional)
Yellow food colouring

Method

Parboil rice with yellow food colouring and set aside. In a pan melt butter, adding sugar, and stirring for a few minutes (ensuring not to overcook), adding nuts, cardamom, orange juice, orange zest, (saffron and pistachio if desired) parboiled rice and a little water just enough to cook it. Seal pot and cook on low heat.

Maintain low heat for 10 to 20 minutes, or until the rice is fluffy and puffed. Enjoy the warmth of simple sweet goodness like none other.

Chapter 6

Frontier

Feasting with the People from the Mountains

Autumn 1995

According to Dadi, history has a strange way of repeating itself, not that most of us know it, or notice it. Though, as she points out, war stories, stories of power and fame, intrigue, murder, manipulation, empires and death are all chronicled in journals, and revealed to generations as 'History Repeats Itself'. However, family stories laced in happiness, love, feast, tragedy, loss, heartache and music get lost in the myopia of time. And, she adds, 'When they return to the same doors knocking, we either let them in, or slam the door on them, not realizing history is repeating itself, again.'

'What happened Dadi?' I ask. 'Why are you going Aristotle on me?' Actually, I know the reason for her sudden philosophical outburst. Of late, Nasreen Phuppo is showing some interest in the comings and goings of Ya Bhai, and Dadi thinks it's because Phuppo wants to arrange a match between Iffat and the eligible owner of B. Bees, and I think so too.

However, there is a minor issue. My cousin, Iffat wants to marry Shahbaz Khan, a classmate at medical school and both are expected to graduate next year, armed with an MBBS degree. I have met Shahbaz several times and he appears to be a fine fellow with a good head on his shoulders, pleasant looking and with a very promising career but Phuppo is unwilling to marry her daughter into a Pathan family, to Dadi's utter chagrin.

Dadi is a forward-thinking woman and judges everyone with one rulebook, while Phuppo is essentially the queen of double standard. She has one rulebook for herself and another for the rest of humanity. Needless to say, Dadi thinks her daughter's approach is reprehensible, and off late is rather obvious about her distaste, to the utmost delight of my mother, Zohra.

My mother, fondly called Ammi by the household and by Ya Bhai and Sofia too, is the backbone of our family. And, interestingly enough, it's not just me who thinks it, it's Dadi's opinion as well, which is rather surprising given the saas/bahu drama the world over. I notice Dadi looking at a photo of Ammi and Phuppo that's hanging on the verandah wall, surely making a comparison. The verandah picture wall is Ammi's latest passion, and every week it seems to grow as newer family photos, old and new are added to the gallery.

Ammi is tall in both stature and presence and mostly talks with her actions and eyes, rather than her words. The only time I've really seen her give way to emotions is when she talks about my excess weight, except for that one time at the beach a decade ago when her calm worked its magic. I've hardly ever heard her talk about my Nani, which is in great contrast to my dad, who talks about his deceased father at the least opportunity.

Knowing my mother's steel and fondness for listening, she is bound to make just one talking point against Nasreen Phuppo's resistance in meeting with Shahbaz's family, annihilating Phuppo's entire case. Dadi and Ammi versus Phuppo, I smile and think of all the possible outcomes of this family drama, and then ask Dadi, 'Have you met Shahbaz?'

'Shahbaz is a wonderful boy,' replies Dadi, as she deshells pine nuts in a bowl for Abbu, and sets them in a glass bowl on the coffee table next to the orange ashtray. 'Iffat introduced me to him a few weeks ago. He was respectful, a little shy I might say, and appeared way beyond his age in wisdom. I was so impressed with his manners, how well-raised the young lad is! I believe his parents are visiting from Peshawar next week and Shahbaz wants them to meet Nasreen and Waheed for a formal introduction. I am completely in favour of this, but your stubborn Phuppo, apparently, has other plans for Iffat, and they include Yahya. I have told her repeatedly that Yahya is not suitable.'

'I hope you did not mention his interest in Sofia, Dadi? Phuppo will tell the entire world, and not only that, she will actually go up to him and ask him why he likes Sofia and not Iffat.' I spring from my rocking chair onto Dadi's daybed, and in my excitement kick the bag of pine nuts, spilling half its contents on the floor.

'Ayesha, why would I tell Nasreen about Yahya's interest in Sofia? I just said he is not suitable, because Iffat's interest lies elsewhere. Pathans are a wonderful people. They *are* a little different from Punjabis, but diversity in a family is a wonderful thing. All that matters is that Shahbaz comes from a cultured, educated, stable background, and is keen to marry Iffat,' says Dadi joining me in picking up the pine nuts.

'What is surprising to me is Nasreen's double standard. At the time of her own courtship some thirty years ago, she insisted on marrying Waheed, who belongs to a Shia-Bohri family, and convinced your Dada, God bless his soul, and I, why it was essential that we give her our blessing and approval, and we did. Initially, your Dada was a little apprehensive, but after listening to her and meeting Waheed and his family he was convinced that it was the right decision to let them get married. But Nasreen seems to have forgotten all that.'

She sounds very exasperated, as she rounds up the last of the spilled pine nuts from the daybed, as I clean the spill from the floor.

'How about we invite Shahbaz's family for dinner to our house, and invite Phuppo and Phuppa too. Maybe if they meet in a neutral setting, things might work out. Plus Abbu is very sweet on boys who are driven, academic and pursuing a career, and could persuade Phuppo to give Shahbaz a chance. Do you think this plan could work?'

Personally, I am convinced that this plan is workable. Abbu is very methodical, logical and professorial when bringing people to his side, especially if he is convinced that he is right. I still remember his prowess in convincing Tayajee Tyyab to allow Ya Bhai to get an MBA degree. He argued Ya Bhai's case with almost the same tenacity as I did, when convincing Sofia to take the Food Stories Global Lahore tour.

The thought of Lahore takes my mind to Faiz and our many topical and animated discussions at Haveli Niazbagh. I remember every minute detail. Why do women focus on the littlest aspects? I ask myself in resignation. Gestures, tone, expression, a fleeting brush of the hand, a little meaningless remark, the same conversation that may mean just a conversation to a man may end up meaning so much more to a woman. Clearly there is no indication from Faiz that he wants to meet again, and here I am, sitting and focusing on tiny details like how he kept finger-combing his hair each time it fell forward.

'Ayesha, Ayesha,' I hear my name from a distance. Lost in thought I look up and see Dadi trying to make conversation with me. 'Can you focus, please. Stop your musing over a cup of tea and concentrate on the matter at hand. I think it's a great idea to entertain Shahbaz's parents here. Let me bring it up with Zohra and get her input.'

If only Dadi knew it's a different kind of musing over a cup of tea that has kept me occupied off late, the one over a tea-trolley pledging Eastern promises. And then as per Dadi's request I decide to focus on the issue at hand, 'Hey Dadi, how about we prepare a Pathan-inspired feast for our guests. Great for conversation and lightening the mood, plus it may serve the dual purpose of making our guests feel important, and seducing Phuppo into agreeing to the match. The taste of the melt-in-the-mouth mutton Karahi, Peshawari chapli kabab, and Kabuli pulao will melt any heart, and Phuppo isn't that bad.'

Hearing my passion for Peshawari food, and my opinion on Phuppo's not so cold heart, the both of us start laughing.

I grab a paper and pencil and get busy making a list of things to do in anticipation of the delightful evening. I hand the paper to Dadi, all the while thinking of my Nani, and the words of Mother Geraldine when she was telling me tales of Convent of Jesus and Mary, Simla. 'Shireen's group of friends was so diversified. Her group consisted of Hindu girls, Sikh girls, Muslim girls, Parsi girls, Christian girls, all hailing from different religions, regions and cultures, but the bond of friendship, love and food always brought them together, especially homemade pulao on Tuesdays. Truth be told, sometimes talking is best left to tradition, customs and food, while we remain silent and watch from the sidelines.'

～

Since my plan to invite Shahbaz's family for dinner was an expected hit at home, I now sit at my regular spot at B. Bees waiting for the takeaway order of Kabuli pulao for the dinner tonight. Dadi and I spent hours setting the formal dining room, coordinating salmon pink cotton napkins to complement the white Wedgewood dinner plates with platinum and salmon-pink edging. The cutlery we lay out is a glistening sterling silver, ornately carved, intricately French in design, and a handful to lift. Needless to say, I have future ownership claims to the flatware. It originally belonged to my great grandmother, later passed on to Nani, and then to Ammi. I am almost certain that half of Salma Khala's interest in wanting me to marry her son is to gain back ownership of the Tiffany cutlery set. It once belonged to her, but no more.

I casually glance at the prearranged stainless steel cutlery on the table at B. Bees and my mind shifts to the sterling silver cutlery at home. I ponder all that it must have tasted and witnessed over the years, the unfolding of joyous occasions and surely some tragic events too. After use, each individual piece is wrapped in tissue, a shade of light turquoise, slipped into clear plastic bubble wrap and stored in a large wooden chest, ornately carved and sitting low on the floor next to the China cabinet in the dining room. The cutlery set is used on rare occasions and hand washed with mild soap, under Dadi's supervision, of course.

Khala had once mentioned to me that the set had originally belonged to Mrs Iris Quail, a British officer's wife, who later gifted it to my great grandmother. Mrs Quail was a friend of the family and moved away from Simla after she caught her husband in bed with her best friend. Before relocating to the British Isles, she gave away all her prized household belongings. I laugh and think of Mother Geraldine aptly quoting, 'The mountain air in Simla breathed promiscuity and every officer seemed to be bedding someone else's wife, making true the statement "every Jack will bed somebody else's Jill".'

I can't help but think that not much has changed over seventy years; married people are still having affairs with others' wives and husbands, formal cutlery is still being pampered more than people's emotions, and delicious food is still being served to reign over people, or to rein people in, and on cue, Haji Sahib signals from behind the cash counter, letting me know that my Kabuli pulao order is ready.

I grab the large bag of takeaway boxes, and hope that our honourable dinner guests tonight enjoy the feast especially prepared for them. Merrily humming along with Steve Perry, the fading sound of 'Don't Stop Believin' playing inside B. Bees, I walk out the double doors and that's when I see him. He's there, some forty feet away. What are the chances of running into Faiz again?

I catch his eyes from behind my sunglasses, but see an odd unfamiliarity to his persona. There is an unrecognizable air to him; he appears the same, but seems different.

I can't help but think, should I acknowledge him or not?

What if he doesn't want to recognize me?

Why would he do that?

He has no reason to ignore me.

Or does he?

Maybe he is preoccupied?

Maybe he wears contact lenses and forgot to wear them and therefore doesn't recognize me from a distance?

He's walking towards the front doors, he's just fifteen-feet away, ten, five, he's passing me by, 'Hi Faiz, good seeing you again,' I say smiling casually and keeping a firm grip on my composure.

'Hi,' he says grinning, and then stops, somehow wanting me to continue the conversation.

'You here to eat biryani?' I ask, and beat myself up on asking a rather silly question, and then continue talking just to appear calm, 'Obviously you are, why else would you be here?'

'Actually, let me not fool you any further,' he says laughing, and stops as though waiting for a reaction from me. I look at him quizzically and wonder how I'm supposed to react. A million possibilities are going through my head. What's he been fooling me about? I can't help but focus on the lyrics of the song playing inside B. Bees.

> *Just a small town girl*
> *Just a city boy...raised in South Detroit...*
> *For a smile they can share the night*
> *It goes on and on, and on...*

Before the silence gets awkward I hear a voice that sounds like mine ask, 'What have you been fooling me about? That you have an evil twin at home?'

He breaks into spontaneous laughter and nods a yes, 'I do have an evil twin at home named Faiz. I'm Zaid, the good twin. This, by far, is the best way I've broken the news to someone that I have a twin.' He can't seem to contain his mirth, but looking at my obvious confusion he stops and asks, 'You didn't know? Faiz is my twin. I'm Zaid, Faiz's younger brother by eleven minutes, and you are?'

'I'm Ayesha and I know Faiz rather formally, therefore I couldn't have known. I'm sorry,' I clarify, not wanting to sound too familiar, or for Zaid to make any assumptions and convey the same to Faiz. I smile noncommittally, wave a casual bye and nice meeting you and turn, breathing a sigh of relief.

'Would you like to have coffee?'

I give myself a few seconds to absorb the question, prepare a reaction and turn. Smiling pleasantly I say, 'Thank you for asking, but I'm in a rush, I have to get home for dinner. Nice meeting you though.'

Did he just ask me for coffee? Yes, I think he did!

A debonair face that looks the same,
A heart not as tender, missing the flame,
The story set in feast has turned a page,
Time has voiced 'action', and the actors are on stage.

∽

The conversation at the table is roaring and the sit-down dinner for twelve is turning out to be unexpectedly pleasant. Our household quorum is complete and my genius in feasting on a Pathan-inspired meal makes a great conversation piece. Uncle Yousuf and Shahana Auntie, Shahbaz's parents, profusely compliment Ammi for her hospitality, and graciously thank Nasreen Phuppo on meeting with them, implying that the match between Iffat and Shahbaz is as good as solemnized.

I playfully kick Iffat under the table, and cringe at the serious expression on Phuppo's face, but she suddenly smiles and humbly responds with a warm, 'The pleasure was all mine, and please honour us with your company for dinner at our home this Saturday evening.'

I squeeze Nadir's arm on my left, he smiles at me, and winks at Iffat and Shahbaz softly whispering a cheesy dialogue at them. 'You two kids, it's time to take this relationship to the next level, and I do not imply what you think I do. All I say is that you can do this now.' Saying so, he grabs Dadi's hand and kisses it affectionately, and to our utter delight Dadi grabs Nadir's face and kisses him on both cheeks, and just as soon as Dadi turns to continue the conversation amongst the elders, Nadir turns to Iffat and mouths, 'You can do that too,' needless to say, the five of us break into spontaneous laughter as Iffat throws a carrot at Nadir.

I look at Nadir, and think of his somewhat delightfully obnoxious ways. He puts on an aura of disdain, but is a gentle soul like Sofia. His career choice of becoming a doctor stems from his desire to help the less fortunate amongst us, and is a testament to his temperament. Sofia distributes money to the less fortunate and Nadir cures them of their ailments without charge. Confident, compassionate, academic and a real ladies man, that's Nadir in a nutshell, and his angular dark looks ensure there is never any dearth of young women surrounding him. As for my relationship with him, he'd push me under a bus if he could, but Dadi thinks just the opposite, 'If there is one person in this world who'll bail you out, it's Nadir, mark my words.'

No Dadi, for once you are wrong, much like the sage or prime minister who advises the ruler, and is unconventionally precise in all evaluations but the most essential. Ours is a sibling rivalry based on an accident of birth and stems from the power struggle, the very power struggle that devastated dynasties before us. I am content with him being the heir apparent, but he is plagued by my survival, by my simplicity of not wanting for more than a tranquil existence, by my unexplainable dichotomous humility sprinkled with arrogance. Yes Dadi, tragically your error in judgement is cloudy because of your undying love for the firstborn, and for that you stand corrected.

The dining table looks magnificent, and the setting and spread are fit to entertain royalty. Plain white cotton silk tablecloth with salmon-pink crochet edging makes for an elegant backdrop to the feast in chapli kabab, Kabuli pulao, mutton karahi, badamjaan raita, and multitude of side dishes and salads. The sterling silver serving platters are oblong and shine as they catch the spotlight falling on the dining table. Ours is a dining room where the spotlights not only highlight the paintings on the walls, but also focus subtle lighting on artistry in cuisine. The Kabuli pulao glistens under the delicate glow of the lamplight, each grain separate from the other, raisin and cashew atop the pulao appear like garnets and topaz, and the soft lamb meat peeks from under the golden rice cover.

Yousuf Uncle draws in a deep breath and spontaneously says, 'Kabuli pulao is considered an ancestor of the Yakhni pulao and my great grandmother told me tall tales about its journey and history. My paternal grandmother was from the Shinwari tribe hailing from Afghanistan, while my maternal grandparents were Afridis. Once, Arminius Vambery, the Hungarian professor was travelling through Herat, en route to Turkey, and stopped for dinner with my great grandfather, and captioned the Kabuli pulao "beautifully flavourful and highly aromatic", and took the recipe with him to journal into his research pertaining to the eating habits of the people of the subcontinent.'

'Uncle, why do people from the North-West Frontier Province and Afghanistan have a diet heavily structured around red meat?' I ask, curious, since he seems to have some knowledge on the issue and may throw some intelligent light on it.

Uncle clears his throat, sips water and across the table I see Shahbaz roll his eyes and shake his head and smile at me. His gesture implying, get ready for a history lecture. I give him a half smile and focus on the lesson, 'In Central Asia and Afghanistan meat was thought to strengthen the core of a man, his valour, strength and virility; hence it was considered the most potent of foods,' he says. 'Food hunting was a way of keeping agile and an effective way of training for battle, therefore rice cooked in meat stock promised a very agreeable mental and physical constitution to the warriors of the region,' he adds. 'The Mughal emperor Babur, a connoisseur of pulao and kababs, on his arrival to the subcontinent complained about the cuisine of the locals and famously penned his views in the *Baburnama*.' He obviously takes great pride in the fact that Babur thought the cuisine of the mountains was superior to that of the rest of Hindustan.

'Apparently, Babur was on an Atkin's diet too,' quips Sameer as light laughter ensues, and then turning to Iffat, he audibly whispers in her ear, 'We have a virile man in the family now,' thankfully only Iffat and I hear that, and she pinches him hard. I hide my smirk, taking refuge behind a glass of water.

'Was it Babur who took the recipe of the pulao with him when he travelled from Central Asia, through Afghanistan and on to India?' I ask, wondering about the role of my ancestors in the migration of the pulao, and before I can get my answer Jalal walks in and quietly whispers something in Nadir's ear. Nadir excuses himself and follows Jalal out.

My eyes fall on the hanging artwork on ivory-coloured walls, all still-life paintings made by Ammi. Her hand is exact and she is able to create a three-dimensional illusion within her artwork, almost giving breath to still life. My favourite is the one displayed on an easel in the far right corner of the room. It's a replication of 'Starry Night over the Rhône' by Dutch painter Vincent Van Gogh. It sits quietly in the corner ruling the room, only drawing attention to itself because of its subtle commanding presence, much like Ammi.

Through the sliding glass doors I see figures stride into the foyer via the verandah entrance, walking into the study left off the main double doors, and then Nadir walks into the dining room and announces, 'Hey Ammi, could you send some chai and dessert to the verandah? Yahya and a few other friends are over.' And then, looking at the younger lot he says, 'You can join us in the verandah, if you want.'

With dinner wrapped up I make my way to my bedroom to take a moment to think about today's events, especially my chance meeting with Faiz's twin brother. I stand at my dresser, brushing my hair and reapplying my lipstick. The shade of the lipstick is a subtle pink-maroon called *Arrogant,* and Sofia insists that Christian Dior named the lipstick defining the likes of me, the untamed kind with subtle natural arrogance. I don't think I'm untamed or arrogant but Sofia insists otherwise.

I walk to the kitchen to get a mug of chai and escape from the side door to the garden up front, resting my head back on the solitary chair and enjoying the sound of laughter from the verandah some distance away. And then I see him, purposefully walking towards me, suddenly I feel a lump in my throat, but thankfully because of the glow of the night lamp the eyes absorb the momentary rush of emotion before any obvious damage to my ego.

'Hi,' he says softly.

'Hi back.'

'How are you?'

'I'm well, and you?'

'I'm well too,' he says smiling.

'Why are you here?'

'Because I have nowhere else to go.'

'Why do you have nowhere else to go?'

'Because I'm here,' he states in a flat voice.

'Oh.'

'Oh good, or oh, not so good?'

'I met your brother today.'

'I know.'

'He asked me out for coffee,' I say softly.

'I know.'

'How do you know?'

'Because he told me.'

'Why would he tell you?' I question.

'Why wouldn't he?'

'Because you don't tell the world when you ask a girl for coffee,' I say beginning to relax.

'What did you say?' He asks, a soft smile playing on his face.

'What do you think I said?'

'I don't know.'

'Why not?' I ask.

'Because I wasn't there.'

'Why weren't you there?'

'Was I supposed to be there?' He whispers.

'I don't know.'

'When will you know?' he asks.

'But he must have told you what I said,' I say softly, deflecting his question.

'You tell me what you said.'

'Why should I?'

'You shouldn't actually,' he says shaking his head and smiling widely, suddenly breaking the tension. He hands me his cup of chai and walks to pull up a chair next to me, sitting down he asks, 'I just met Shahbaz on your verandah, he was a few years junior to me at school. How do you know him?'

I feel like saying *that's a great question,* like all politicians, and silently thank him for giving me the opportunity to ramble for a few minutes. I hear my voice from a distance, and slowly through talking and gestures put my calm back together again, telling him the entire dinner episode including Nadir's and Sameer's antics, Yousuf Uncle's remarks about virility, masculinity and meat, and finally concluding with, 'I think it's the Kabuli pulao that did the trick, I think once Phuppo had her first bite of it, she was as good as sold on the idea of Iffat and Shahbaz getting married. And to think, we wasted all these years trying to convince her to meet with Shahbaz's family. All it took was a bite of pulao.' I notice Faiz looking on with amusement.

'Can I have another cup of chai? This one's cold?' he asks, pouring the cold chai in the grass.

'Sure, you want to go to the verandah and sit with everyone else, and maybe eat some dessert as well?'

'I think it's nicer here, *Under the Greenwood Tree*,' he says pointing to the large tree in the corner of the garden and then goes on to recite the entire poem. 'William Shakespeare, *As You Like It*,' he says winking at me.

I throw my head back and start laughing, utterly delighted and charmed at the sweet rendition and apt timing of the recitation, 'That was so charming.'

'I remember it from school, and every time I'm in the vicinity of a lush tree, the poem just slips out,' he says smiling, as the both of us get up to get ourselves fresh chai from the trolley in the verandah.

❧

I pick up my fourth slice of pizza and eat it, fast. Sameer shakes his head and says, 'What's with this gluttony? You're tiny, it's shocking to see you eat so much in one sitting. How much have you eaten, and since when have you been starving yourself?'

'I'm so hungry I could eat another large slice, and garlic bread too. Someone stop me.'

Nadir is sitting quietly observing us. He knows I am an emotional eater and I bet he's wondering what it is that is bothering me so much. According to him, I have immense mental strength, as shown by my conquering obesity at a very young age. He has not seen me eat the way I have in the last twenty-four hours with gusto and gluttony, in at least a decade. And off late I admit my obsessive regimen with exercise is looking lukewarm too. Nadir is not worried about my gaining weight, but about what is driving my odd behaviour. He gets up and says, 'Hey Ash, let's go for dinner, just you and me, say what you?'

'Nadir, are you asking me out? I'm your sister,' I reply, tossing a dirty tissue at him. Sameer joins me in lobbing wadded-up tissues and then asks, 'Nadir Bhai, why are you only asking her out, what about me, I'm overeating too.'

'Oh, shut up both of you. What's bothering you Ash?'

'You,' I snap wanting to stop that line of questioning. Then to divert Nadir I say, 'Sofia is insisting the "Life's a Beach" series should be based purely on photography, while I think a blue and white sketch on the cards will make for a great concept too. And since I'm not used to disagreeing with Sofia the tension at the office is taking a toll. I think it's driving me towards food and away from exercise.'

And I pat myself on the back for my artistry and flawless delivery, and make a mental note of updating Sofia about my loop of lies. How do liars lie all the time? Perhaps we should come up with a line of greeting cards for liars that say, '*To cover a lie, you embark on an unpleasant journey of lies. And remember it's never about the destination, only about the unpleasant lies you spin on your way.*'

∼

I sit in my rocking chair, going back and forth, it's been forty-eight hours since the night in the garden and there has been no sign of Faiz. If he was interested he would have made an appearance by now.

I keep rocking my chair and count the number of times I can rock in one minute. Somewhere in the background I hear a dog bark, a plane fly by, a ship blow its horn a few miles off the shores of Clifton Beach, and the home phone ring. All the other sounds stop but the home phone keeps ringing. It rings persistently and then finally stops. I feel myself dozing off and make my way to Dadi's daybed. Covering myself with a crisp cotton sheet and getting ready for a quick nap, I hear the phone ring again. I get up to answer it. Maybe it's Faiz.

Disappointed, I settle on the daybed again, and just then I see Ammi walk in through the front gate, 'Hey Ammi, someone just called for you.'

'Who?'

'Mehreen!'

'Mehreen who?' she asks.

I shrug my shoulders, roll my eyes and doze off to a world of better dreams.

The world of daydreams isn't happy any more.

∾

KABULI PULAO, PRIDE OF THE NORTH

The uncomplicated joys of childhood and the glee that comes with enjoying the simple pleasures of eating; what a wonderful state of mind happy nostalgia brings, and how lucky we are to relive it time and again.

Interestingly Kabuli pulao is a delicious blend of savoury and sweet, the subtle sweetness and crunchiness of fried carrots and raisins adds an oomph to the mild saltiness of the rice and meat, while the texture of almonds, pistachios and cashews bring a richness to the flavour that is unique in taste and texture. Research leads us to believe that carrots were indigenous to Afghanistan for millennia, as were grapes, raisins and other kinds of dry fruits; therefore, the chefs of the times and the region may have used these particular ingredients in the Kabuli pulao because they were the perfect combination of easy availability and sophisticated taste, laden with what was thought to be superior food.

Ingredients

2 ½ lb chicken or goat meat
2 small onions
1 tsp ginger
1 tsp garlic
2 tsp black cumin
½ cup oil
Salt to taste
1 tsp garam masala
2 mugs rice
½ cup raisins
½ cup cashewnuts
½ cup almonds
3 grated carrots
½ tsp sugar

Method

Heat oil adding meat, ginger and garlic and fry for a few minutes. Add sliced onions and stir until meat changes colour, then add black cumin, garam masala powder and salt. Fry for a few minutes, adding seven to eight mugs of water, reducing to half the quantity or until the meat is tender. Add ¼ cup raisins, cashews and almonds to the stock.

Once the meat is tender add pre-washed rice to the cooking broth. Maintain high heat until rice fluffs and the stock is a thin layer on the top. Transfer to an oven-resistant dish, seal dish and put into preheated oven (medium to low heat) for 20 to 30 minutes.

In a frying pan heat two to three tablespoons of oil, pour sugar, add grated carrots and remaining raisins, cashew and almonds, stir fry for a minute and use as garnish on top of the pulao. Your Kabuli pulao is ready to be served.

◆

MUTTON KARAHI (KARAHI GOSHT)

Karahi gosht is said to be a dish of the NWFP. In the city of Peshawar, and its surrounding areas, meat rules as it does in all the other provinces of Pakistan. Historically speaking, lamb and goat meat (mutton) has always been a favoured meat of South Asia, the Middle East, Central Asia and the Mediterranean. Maybe it was the availability of the animal, or its size that caused it to be hunted as a quick and easy dinner, or the fact that goat and lamb meat is the most deliciously tender and juicy meat—but I am biased since mutton happens to be my favourite meat of choice.

How did the traditional lamb karahi come to be? My research pointed me to Landi Kotal, a rustic and traditionally Pukhtoon town, sitting close to Afghanistan atop the Khyber Pass. The Shinwari and Afridi tribes hail from this region and it is also considered to be the historical home of the balti or karahi gosht. The karahi gosht is named after the utensil it is cooked in, the 'balti' or 'karahi' (the cooking utensil 'balti' is referred to as 'karahi' in southern Pakistan) are somewhat similar; both are heavy-based round wok-like pots. From Landi Kotal, the delicious balti gosht travelled to Punjab, thus spreading to the rest of the world.

Mutton karahi is simple and fabulous all at once, small cubes of lamb or goat cooked in tomatoes, green chillies, salt and preferably animal fat. The fresh meat is thought to provide the fat base for the cooking, and it is meant to be savoured directly from the karahi with a side of hot naan.

My father travelled frequently with his job, and on one of his ventures he travelled to Landi Kotal and got the recipe right from its city of origin.

Ingredients

4 lb goat leg, cut in small cubes
2 lb tomatoes
7 to 10 green chillies or to taste (chopped)
Salt to taste
Oil ½ cup, but with fresh qurbani meat the animal fat should suffice

Method

Braise meat on high heat, adding green chillies and salt, cook for a few minutes adding tomatoes. Cook until meat is tender and tomato juice has evaporated through cooking, and the now orange-red tender meat is ready to be served with hot delicious naan. Eid mubarak, have a blessed one.

◆

CHAPLI KABAB

My cousin was a cadet at the Kimari Naval Base, and most of his weekends were spent at our home. The best part of his visit to our house was the drop off to the Kimari Naval Base, for on the way back my parents invariably made a stop at the Chapli Kabab Dhaaba.

Come every Saturday morning, my anticipation for dinner that night knew no bounds. I could taste the scrumptious kabab, the flavour of the anardana or pomegranate, and tomatoes wrapped in hot naan.

Kabab, is an ancient food, and has travelled far and wide through regions, and times, to become a universal food. It is undoubtedly the most recognized eastern food in the western part of the world, and a real favourite with desis, middle easterners, Arabs, central Asians and Caucasians alike. It is believed that Turkish and Persian soldiers enjoyed grilling seasoned and fresh meat on fire, while it hung wrapped on their swords. Kababs have always been a royal and rustic favourite, and though they were said to be on the Mughal menu, the variation of the modern day chapli kabab is a purely Phustoon and Peshawari delight. Therefore, the Frontier province, and the region of Afghanistan can proudly lay claim to it.

The word kabab is said to originate from the Arabic language, but the Persians, Turks and central Asians also lay claim to it. It means to fry, burn or cook on a skewer through grilling or open fire cooking.

Chapli kabab is a spicy, flat meat patty and is said to be a treat from the eastern part of Afghanistan, and of course our very own Peshawar; it is a favourite all over Pakistan and India. Chaprikh is a *Pashto* word meaning flat, and chapli is a derivation of this particular word; hence a flat, round kabab, served with yogurt and naan. The Pukhtoon recipe uses a perfect combination of meat and atta (wheat flour), thus the kabab is lighter in taste and on the pocket.

The ingredients used in the preparation of chapli kababs are indigenous to Afghanistan. Therefore, the use of pomegranate seeds and dry coriander seeds, which make it unique in taste, are more a gift of nature than a deliberate effort of the chefs creating this recipe.

Ingredients

1 lb ground meat, lamb, goat, chicken or beef
4 tbsp whole wheat flour
1 medium onion, chopped
1 tsp chilli powder
1 tsp cumin

1 tsp garam masala powder
Salt to taste
4 tbsp fresh cilantro
2 green chillies, chopped
1 tbsp coriander seeds, crushed
½ egg
1 tsp anardana
1 tbsp oil
½ tsp baking powder
2 medium tomatoes, chopped
Oil for frying

Method

Mix ingredients in a large bowl, make flat patty, and shallow fry to enjoy with naan and dahi.

❧

Chapter 7

Beach

The Waves of Life

Certain situations in life become banal because people gravitate towards recreating them again and again, and despite circumstances being hackneyed, time seems to derive satisfaction in putting us through the 'same ole same ole', in essence, thriving on clichés. Therefore, sitting on my rocking chair feeling forlorn, and listening to a ballad about unrequited love I make a pathetic picture, and can easily be sold in the cliché section of Musings Over a Cup of Tea.

I have fallen in love and am shamelessly admitting to it.

I don't know what else to call it.

I don't know how to describe it.

I don't know what to do with it.

All I know is that I feel it.

How would I best describe my state of mind if my life depended on it?

Unrequited love is a back-and-forth between cognitive frenzy and cerebral despair, that's the best I can come up with. My unrequited love schedule is predictably boring. I wake up in the morning, have chai, go to work, pretend to work, arrive home to probing eyes, get into my comfy clothes, usually a worn out cotton outfit, sit in my rocking chair, and listen to a wide selection of pathetically sad songs in English, Spanish, Urdu, Hindi, Punjabi, Sindhi and Italian. Out of the seven, three languages I do not understand, but the music and soulful rendition of the lyrics are rather self-explanatory and a real booster to the pathetic aura surrounding me. My current favourite is 'Nothing without You', commonly known as 'Sajna Teray Bina' sung by Nusrat Fateh Ali Khan. Since his collaboration with Peter Gabriel on the musical score of *The Last Temptation of Christ*, Nusrat Fateh Ali Khan's popularity and international fame had soared, and many of his song lyrics now come with an English translation. And needless to say, since I can hold a tune decently well, my personal rendition of the incomparable 'Ranjish hi Sahi', written by Ahmed Faraz, and 'Aaj Jaane ki Zid Na Karo' written by Fayyaz Hashmi, is now as good as it gets.

I end my days by either going to sleep on an empty stomach, or indulging in a feast of gluttony.

Luckily, Ammi left to visit with her brother in London three days after the lavish feast she hosted for Shahbaz's parents, and Dadi has shifted to Phuppo's house for a week. Therefore, it's just the men and me. Sameer is too self-involved to care, Nadir has very long hours at the hospital, but has been giving me quizzical glances ever so often, Abbu is too busy at work to notice, and Jalal has his hands full looking after the kitchen and the house. Hence my comings, goings, eating and starving remain unnoticed.

It's been more than a week since my last encounter with Faiz, and I wonder if I'll ever see him again, or maybe see him in circumstances that I would prefer to see him in? The mere thought is exhilarating. In reality since it took me almost twenty-four years to meet him the first time, maybe it'll take another twenty-four to meet him again. I pour myself a glass of water from the kitchen and head to my room in anticipation of turning in early when I hear the phone ring.

'Hello.'

'Hello, could I speak to Zohra?' asks a rather melodious voice on the other side.

'She is away. Could I take a name and a number, and have her call you back?'

'Sure, but I called a couple of days ago as well. When will she be back?'

'She is travelling abroad and will return in a couple of weeks. Could I ask who's calling and take a message?' I repeat my earlier request.

'This is Mehreen. Am I speaking to Ayesha?'

She knows my name, and I have no idea who she is, 'Yes it is, could I take a message?' I ask for the third time, but with no success.

'I'll call her back in a few weeks. Thank you and bye,' she says hanging up.

I scribble her name on a scratchpad next to the phone and head back to my room shutting the noise out. The phone rings again as I turn up the volume on 'Nothing without You' and get into a comfortable position in the hopes of a chance dream encounter. And then Jalal comes knocking.

'Yes?' I ask.

'It's Jalal, someone is calling for you, and I have the cordless here.'

Taking the phone and tripping on my hairbrush, which is a perpetual feature on the floor, I say, 'Hi.'

'Hi Ayesha,' says the voice on the other end of the line. Is it Faiz, or Zaid?

It could be Zaid, he's the one who asked me for coffee. He sounds different, his voice a little deeper than I recall it being.

What if it's Faiz? However, assumptions are said to be the mother of all big screw-ups, and I refrain from any expectation, or glorious presumption.

'I'm well, who's this?' I ask focusing on the delivery of my words, rather than my emotion.

'Who do you think it is?' asks the voice. I can hear subtle amusement, which is a little annoying, since I'm at a disadvantage due to my lack of knowledge as to which brother I'm speaking with.

'I don't know? Moeed Mir?' I ask, letting my state of mind get the better of me.

'Yes, Moeed Mir,' comes an unperturbed and surprising response, leaving me just a little confused as to what my comeback should be. However, I'm not one to back down easy.

'Hi Moeed, how can I help?' I ask, hoping his answer will give him away.

'I called to ask if you want to go for dinner tonight? If not, then I was hoping to come over and see you?' The question is like an onion, with multiple peels, but thankfully gives away the identity of the pursuer.

My parents aren't home, my brothers aren't home, and Dadi is away too. And Eastern culture, laced in traditional values, nuances and unwritten observances, states that an unattached young woman must not go out, or invite a young man into her space, without understanding his intention. Sensible conservative values and balanced liberal morality are the cornerstones of Eastern romances as they build to a courtship. However, as much as I appreciate the rationality of this principle, I am torn by my sentiments and want to invite him over, or step out of bounds with him. I stare at the cordless phone in my hand, my reflection in the dresser mirror, at the glass of water on the dresser, and the CD cover reading, 'includes Nothing without You by the living legend Nusrat Fateh

Ali Khan, now featuring Peter Gabriel'.

Putting the phone to my ear I ask, smiling, 'First you have to tell me who you are.'

'I'm whoever you want me to be,' comes the response.

'Faiz, I'll meet you at nine-thirty for dinner, and I'll come as myself.'

And then he starts laughing, and I start laughing, and just as suddenly there is a power breakdown stopping 'Nothing without You' in its tracks and leaving behind only the sound of laughter, and the sound of music by the rhythmic beat of life.

～

The lobby is packed, but it's easy to spot him, his casual elegance hard to miss. However, the first thing I notice are his eyes, baby brown and smiling, the crisp white cotton shirt with rolled sleeves, tucked into blue denim over tan-coloured suede ankle boots. I smile to mask my nervousness and am greeted with a smile. He casually glances my way before turning his attention to the restaurant host.

I've taken care, dressing up in a plain white cotton ensemble, unbraided long hair and a whole lot of *Arrogant,* in attitude and on the smile. Obviously Sophia knows me better than I know myself. We settle at our table for two, and I'm entirely oblivious to my surroundings. I consider myself an expert at keeping nervous excitement at bay. It's something I mastered as an overweight child. I vividly remember each time the conversation would veer towards my excess physical baggage I would hide behind a glass of water and sip my trepidation away, or when a delicious feast beckoned, I would pretend a casual disdain for the offering.

I silently call out to my little self from the past for a quick tutorial in confidence.

Faiz appears forbidden territory, almost like the sumptuously delicious chocolate cake I desperately wanted to eat as an overweight child. The very cake I have forever wanted to have and eat, concurrently. And now, unexpectedly, the cake is offering itself to me; it's enticing, inviting, tempting and with each moment my anticipation of tasting its lusciousness is growing, but so is my apprehension. I hear an inner voice whispering, *this is too good to be true, there has to be a catch, remember, you can't have your cake and eat it too.* And then he asks the unexpected, 'Your mother is travelling?'

'Yes, how do you know? I haven't told you, have I?'

I'm taken aback by his question, and look at him questioningly, his eyes answer one way while his words another, 'No, you haven't.'

And then in a moment of instinctive clarity I realize how he knows. Very calmly I move the conversation forward, pretending ignorance, unwittingly aware that ignorance is bliss.

~

Dark knight

I sit at the beach, alone, tired and hungry. And suddenly I need my mother, but she is nowhere to be found, she is in a far-off land unwilling to listen while there is so much here that needs her attention. Trust her to run off to the land of kings and queens when her guidance is required in abundance amongst her own.

The temper of the autumn sea is placid and sleepy; almost boring, and I have no penchant to deceive myself into thinking that this calm is a cover for serene. It's the unemotional before the emotional, numb before the breakdown, calm before the storm.

My emotions have caught me entirely off guard. I am unaware of how much I've intrigued him, but I've obviously piqued his attention, and while this is a promising start, it is in no way a predictor of a pathway to a successful love story. It's taken him five months to invite me to dinner, while it took his brother five minutes.

And maybe that was the toss decider?

I've obviously charmed him some and should be overly enthusiastic in casting a spell, but there is a cloud of premonition, a strong feeling of déjà vu, an air of uncertainty I can't shirk off.

Why?

Shouldn't I be doing a waltz to the 'Blue Danube', or a bhangra-style Punjabi dance to celebrate the reality that my interest is not unrequited?

Yes, that is what conventional wisdom dictates.

Do I think I'm unlovable, hence my trepidation?

No, that can't be it since I'm not lacking in confidence.

Do I fear someone loving me, losing me, and in the process getting hurt, therefore my angst?

No, I'm stable in my decisions, and am confident in the realization that I would not walk out on someone on a whim.

Do I fear loving someone and the vulnerability it brings?

No, such is not my personality. I have forever worshipped the idea of *falling in love*.

Then what is it that is bringing forth my apparent unease?

'Nani, Nani, Nani!' My gaze follows the voice. It's a toddler running after an older woman and calling out to her. The woman looks like the little boy's grandmother. Suddenly she stops in her tracks breaking the toddler's momentum as he bumps into her. She picks him up, plants a kiss on his forehead and asks, 'Why are you running after me?' I have my answer. I need to know Nani's story. What happened to her?

Why does no one talk about her?

How is she connected to me?

Why am I running after her without knowing her story?

Do I owe her something?

Maybe she is my missing link.

My unfounded conjecture brings forth an aura of calm and I feel like myself again. Far at a distance Ajit and Sofia are gainfully occupied with the camera lens. He is running after seagulls, focusing his camera lens on jagged rocks, the wide sea, a solitary ship on the horizon, sand castles in the air and on the beach, and a silhouette of my pathetic self. She is playing the art director guiding him to the perfect shot worth a thousand words.

The sun is getting ready to set and Ajit captures shots of the dying embers and the golden hues it's leaving behind. I see him getting excited about dusk, his favourite photography hour of the day. His excitement is infectious and he captures my profile on the heels of sultry lighting, captioning it, 'Waiting for a dark knight'.

Nadir and Imran are busy getting the bonfire ready, while Jalal and Haji Chacha are grilling trays on the barbecue. I see Ya Bhai's car pull up, as do cauldrons of food, drinks and ice. Every few minutes a car pulls up, and friends and cousins are arriving in groups of twos and threes. The photography shoot-cum-family beach night has turned into a big party without me being aware of it. The mingled aroma of chicken tikka, Bihari kabab, and seekh kabab are playing havoc with my hungry insides. The succulent Bihari kabab is made using a recipe my Nani's cook brought back with him from Bihar at the time of the great migration in 1947.

The recipe has nourished my family through country, and family wars, and though Salma Khala is not one to share recipes, this one made it out of her vault thanks to Jalal's persuasive ways. He convinced Khala's cook to share the recipe, insisting that Bihari kabab is a purely Bihari and Bengali take on the kabab, hence the recipe must be shared amongst people hailing from those regions.

I invariably smile thinking of Jalal's persuasive powers, and his excitement at breaking the news to us some years ago:

I gave Salma Khala's cook a long speech about the history of the Bihari kabab; I said the subcontinent hosts more than a dozen popular kabab recipes—shami, reshmi, dum, boti, seekh, chapli, galavati, tandoori and the Bihari kabab, amongst many. But the uniqueness of the Bihari kabab is in its masala, texture, marinade and spice content. And though cuisine from Bihar is traditionally vegetarian, the Bihari kabab not so much. It is a meat delight that has an infusion of mustard oil, largely used in India, and specifically Bengal and Bihar, and a liberal amount of masalas. The use of kabab chini, poppy seeds, nutmeg, mace and papaya as the meat tenderizer gives it its melt-in-the-mouth tenderness. The secret ingredient is a generous addition of Bihari kabab garam masala.

I remember Dadi's delight at the unfolding of the Bihari kabab episode, and her magnanimous declaration that she was surrendering to Jalal's expertise in all things kitchen, 'Jalal, you have finally proved your mettle in the kitchen, and I now promise to call Palla fish, Hilsa. Did you ask for the Ungushti recipe?'

'Ungushti, what the heck is that?' I asked.

'Ungushti is a delight made with leftover Bihari kabab marinade. The marinade is folded into a generous helping of flour, tightly wrapped on skewers, and grilled to golden perfection,' I recall Dadi's words as I sit at the beach waiting for my delicious plate of barbecued meat with a side of ungushti.

Ephemeral smoke curling from the grill and exuding from it the appetizing aroma of the spicy chicken tikka, and Bihari kabab makes me dizzy with hunger. The yogurt-infused spice soaks the flesh in its seductive embrace deepening the zest of the bite, bringing forth its succulent texture. I decide to let the appetite build further and to dine later in the night with a larger group of friends. And though my spot next to the bonfire is cozy, I head to the front porch of the hut in the hopes of socializing the night away.

The raised verandah is large and airy, open on three sides, except for the side attached to the hut. Loungers are occupied, chit-chat is loud, music is subtle, and the laughter wonderfully pleasant. Every couple of feet there is a hug and a 'how are you', and the overwhelming smell of food, noise and hunger is creating an almost heady sensation. I decide to grab a plate of food and head back to the bonfire. Enjoying my solitude, gazing the skies, relishing my hunger, humming 'Aitebaar' by *Vital Signs*, and captioning tonight 'the perfect evening' in my head.

I hear quiet footsteps and smell his cologne before I see him, and dramatically throw my arms up in the air for him to pull me to my feet, twirling theatrically on the uneven sandy surface I declare, 'Oh Mr Darcy, you came, you came. How wonderfully ardent of you to follow me around like this. Might I infer the delightfully obvious from this encounter? Might I, kind sir?' He looks at me and breaks into laughter, unabashedly and with abandon. Gone are my fears for the moment, maybe to return tomorrow, and once again cliché is at play. Logic and intellect play second fiddle to adrenaline, and I willingly surrender.

Maybe it's the sensuous effect of his cologne, the impact of food on my empty stomach, the magic of the bonfire, the enchanting starry, starry night, the thrill of youth, or just my God-given personality, but I deliberately decide to throw caution to the wind, and see where it takes me.

We head on to the porch where the feast is on. Faiz creates a meat fest on his plate, while I decide to indulge on a thick, moist, sweet, velvety and devilishly delicious slice of chocolate cake. Greeting and meeting along the way, we make our way to the bonfire and find a sandy spot optimally close to feel the heat of the embers, but assuredly distant to avoid a burn. I gaze at the sky and catch the crescent moon looking sleek, curvy and enchanting, alluring me to hop on for a joyride, perhaps a swing in its lap.

'Do you think Mohammed Bin Qasim entered the subcontinent from this very coast? I always wonder.'

'There is so much conjecture on the exact location of Debal. The Arabs apparently entered the Indus Delta arriving at a prosperous pirate stronghold, and thought it the most thriving economic hub of South Asia. Many believe that this economic centre was Debal. It is believed to be some twenty miles south-west of Thatta. So much research has been done to find an exact location of Mohammed Bin Qasim's entry point, but there is no popular consensus, or agreement on the exact location. Since all recorded history was written after the fact, no one really knows. Have you read *Arabian Nights*?' he asks.

'Nope.'

'There is a mention of a booming port in India, in the story of Zobeide. Many believe that to be Debal. How true that is, your guess is as good as mine and Ibn Batutta's. The great traveller was very curious about its precise whereabouts too, as are you,' he says smiling, and then looks to the open sea and continues, 'Look at Pakistan's coastline, it's so full of promise, almost eleven-hundred kilometres lining the northern Arabian Sea, and so much of it going to waste.'

'I had some weight issues as a child,' I reply. 'And so every morning I went for a walk with my parents. Just as surely as the sun rises in the East I would rise, put on my sneakers and be waiting downstairs in the foyer for either of my parents to take me for a walk. The beach is a short distance from the house, you've seen it of course, we'd be at the beach in a few minutes and I'd walk to the end of Sea View Apartments. Beyond that were marshes and bushes, and each time I tried to peek through, my dad would say, if you walk a few hundred miles to the south-east you'll hit Bombai, and a few hundred miles to the West, you'll hit the pristine beaches of Baluchistan. Just the notion was so fascinating to me,' I say whimsically.

'Did you ever try?'

'So clever, aren't you?'

He winks, nods his head and asks, 'How's the cake, looks delicious.'

'It is, but it's all mine, I'm not sharing,' I say moving my plate away from his reach, and then continue, 'And to think that the people who must have landed with Mohammed Bin Qasim on Debal, must have barbecued food like us, and eaten it and chatted on the beach, before they attacked Raja Dahir,' I say laughing.

'They weren't eating barbecue or chocolate cake!'

'Yes, they were eating barbecue. Fire is elemental, and as humans we love the smokiness that comes with grilling foods. It goes back millennia, to the beginning of time,' I declare rather passionately.

'Naturally, evolution taught us to cook with fire, that doesn't necessarily mean we were barbecuing Bihari kabab and chicken tikka,' he says, particularly amused by my earlier outburst.

I start chuckling, soaking in the sensuous night. Faiz gets up, pulling me to my feet as we head to the verandah to get chai. Expectedly the teapots are empty, and I grab a soda bottle instead to load up on caffeine. Faiz insists on having both, chai and soda, and requests for a cup, which Ajit volunteers to make. Handing Faiz chai, Ajit looks at me grinning and asks, 'Dark knight?'

'No full moon tonight, and the crescent vanished too, therefore a dark night it is,' replies Faiz, obviously inferring the moonless night.

I chuckle at Faiz's response, look Ajit square in the eyes and answer his question as best as I know, 'Not so elementary my dear Watson, it's not so elementary after all.'

～

Bribery is a dichotomy. While it is obviously detrimental, damaging and destructive to the workings of big government, big business, and life itself, factually it is what fills the stomach of the poor of the Third World. And it is with some relevance that I can now proudly claim my admittance into the detestable and acceptable corrupt system that runs the mechanics of my young nation.

I sit inside the grand grounds of the Mohatta Palace, sketching the home built by Shivratan Mohatta for his beloved wife. A castle of sorts, the home is sealed to the public, but like everything else, getting access to the entrance of the derelict palace has a price. And once the price is negotiated and satisfied we find our humble selves inside the gates of the home.

I pass this splendid home almost every day and wonder about the lives that lived and perished here. The palatial home is said to have been the summer abode of Shivratan Mohatta's family, and played the part from 1927 until the partition of 1947.

Measuring the hot and humid summers of Karachi, it is fatiguing to imagine that my city could play a pleasant host in the summer, but Dadi claims otherwise. She insists that the city's population explosion, industrial revolution, vehicular traffic and construction have altered its summer temperatures, and talks with much pleasure about its climate from the days of yore.

She insists that balmy evenings of Karachi, its metropolitan aura, cosmopolitan lifestyle, business savvy, and reputation for being a modern port city, entirely independent in mindset from the landlocked Punjab, made it a perfect location to build a summer home in. Dadi being a diehard Karachiite lives by the mantra, 'Punjab may have the five rivers, but we have the Arabian Sea, and there is no better land than one next to the sea.'

Though the mansion is decaying, the fountains dry and the once lavish lawns neglected, the magnificent Rajput palace flanked in pink Jodhpur stone and ochre Gizri stone must have been a spectacular sight to be welcomed into, and splendid to call home in the days when it operated as a residence. Much like a beautiful woman, most glorious and glamorous when cherished by the one she loves.

The old man sitting by the guard walks with us, giving us the best kind of history lesson, unmarred by textbooks and soaked in experience. He walks the grounds, pointing to the once-used tunnel that runs under the grounds of the grand residence leading to a temple Mrs Mohatta used for her daily worship.

The grand façade, though dilapidated and neglected, promises tales of a happy time when a prosperous family must have lived here with their barrage of servants, horses, carriages and children, hosting bridge parties, tea parties and dinners abounding with family, friends and food.

The blue and red entrance is in rich contrast to the pink and yellow stone structure, sitting opposite the large dirt ground that must have once been a lush lawn, with gushing fountains, blooming trees, fragrant flowers and merry birds.

The old guard talks nostalgically about the original owners of the house, and their passion for all structures Indo-Gothic. The inspiration to construct the grand home came from all structures designed in the Indo-Saracenic format, both government and private, that were built at the time of the British Raj to elevate the perception that the imperialists were unconquerable. The analogy reminds me of the sham of invincibility I carry in my youth, my unfounded fallacy in the actuality that nothing can ever go wrong.

Nani must have felt the same sentiments, as do all youth, and my mind wanders to my recent conversation with Mother Geraldine about her once happy student named Shireen. It was on Sophia's suggestion that I decided to seek my old principal, and her knowledge on Nani's silent and unfinished legacy.

My visit with Mother Geraldine got me vague answers about my deep-rooted genetic connection to Nani, and also my mother's irrational fears that I would end up like her mother. 'Shireen [Nani] looked much like you when I knew her,' said Mother Geraldine, 'especially now that you have lost weight. However, what is interesting is that she was slim and beautiful in her adolescence and young adulthood, while it is the opposite for you Ayesha. You were an overweight child and seem to have lost all the extra weight and matured into a lovely young woman.'

'What is it that you mean by opposite Mother Geraldine?' I asked perplexed by the conversation and the direction it seemed to be taking.

'Your grandmother was a happy child,' she said. 'She graduated school and moved to Delhi a year before the partition of 1947. I never saw her after her graduation, but heard many conflicting stories about her. I believe she fell in love with a man, but could never marry him. He left her at the altar, and she had to marry her cousin instead,' said Mother Geraldine.

'Last I heard she moved to Pakistan after the 1947 partition, developed mental health issues, suffered a nervous breakdown, battled obesity and eventually died at a very young age. I often wondered if her life would have been different had she married the man she loved.'

Maybe it was best that Nani's story had not been revealed to me, now I knew too much. Sitting on a broken bench at Mohatta Palace, contemplating the reality of my genetics, and the fictitious romantic tales I had spun around my Nana and Nani, I realize that the story of the tragic tale of Shireen and Khusro, from millennia past, had come true once again.

The romantic ballad written by the Persian poet Nizami Ganjavi focusing on the love story of Shireen and Khusro, however tragic, always gave me hope, since I passionately believed in the love story of my maternal grandparents, who went by the same name. And to now acknowledge their reality is mournful. Nani never loved Nana, but loved another. Instead I should have focused on the version written by Amir Khusro, of the Masnavi Shireen-o-Khusro, where he created great mystery and suspense in Shireen's doomed love story with the other man, namely Farhad!

The obese beginning of my life was the obese end of Nani's, and maybe I was cursed with the baggage of her weight at a young age, to pay a debt. Possibly she is my missing link, her gluttonous love affair with food, unfulfilled desires, and unrequited romance is a story I'm meant to complete.

However my assumption has many flaws, it is simple, dispassionate and does not satiate my quest for finding satisfactory answers. Maybe I'm not meant to find answers, only meant to live my life making choices that may *not* become a burden on the generations following me.

I make my way to Sofia. She is standing by a headless, dry water fountain, caressing it lovingly as if feeling its pain. She turns to me and says, 'I recommend that you don't feel hurt for your

Nani. In essence her not being able to marry the man she loved is what makes your existence possible. Be grateful for it.'

However tragic, it is the truest thing I've heard in a while. Our life choices determine everything. Had circumstances allowed Nani to marry the man she loved, life's actuality might not have included me, and so many surrounding me.

We inherit some choices, some we make,
Lessons we learn, some we break,
Celebration of love is a blessing so divine,
Bonds of passion must anticipate the perfect time.

~

CHICKEN TIKKA

Karachi does chicken tikka like no city on the planet, and that is as true as the sun setting in the Arabian Sea off the coast of Karachi. Hence growing up in the wonderful metropolis I have had the luxury of tasting the best barbecue available to man. Expectedly, each trip to my favourite barbecue joint has me devouring tender chicken tikka off the bone. One hand tearing at the warkhi paratha, while the other is busy dipping thinly sliced onions in tamarind chutney, and the result is my taste buds enjoying a meal in foodopia.

The history of grilling meat goes back millennia and we can safely assume that our ancestors were grilling meats from the very beginning of time; when they burnt themselves with fire. Travelling men hunted and cooked meat over fire, sometimes rubbing salt water, or available herbs on it. My research also led me to understand that barbecuing and grilling are entirely different; until now I thought the two were each an interchangeable form of cooking. Grilling is the cooking of raw foods in its basic form over direct fire or heat source, while barbecuing is slow cooking over indirect heat. Hence this slow cooking process infuses the barbecued meats with a delicious smokiness of the charcoal (if used as a heat source) and marinade.

The wonderfully rich subcontinent has a large menu encompassing traditional meat items. Countries like Pakistan, India, Bangladesh, Nepal, Sri Lanka and other regional countries are more alike culturally than different, and the availability of spices, meats, dairy, fruits, vegetables and grains has played a key role in the evolution of the subcontinental cuisine.

Ingredients

10 chicken legs (whole) with barbecue cuts (skin off)
1 cup yogurt
2 to 3 tbsp red chilli powder (or to taste)
Salt to taste
6 to 8 tbsp lemon juice
½ tsp ajwain roasted and ground
Red food colour ¼ to ½ tsp

Method

Combine all ingredients (except chicken) to make the marinade, mix well, let sit for 10 minutes. Marinate chicken and refrigerate 6 to 8 hours. Grill on a barbecue grill or bake in an oven, periodically brushing with oil. Once tender, charcoal the tikka to get the desired smoky flavour. Serve with side of yogurt, tamarind chutney, sliced onions and naan.

♦

TANDOORI CHICKEN

Cooking is not about exact measurements, exact techniques, or exact cooking time, instead it is the 'art with heart' of somewhat following a recipe, going with approximates and tweaking it if required. If tomatoes are not available, find a substitute, or not; turmeric, cumin, coriander or any spice label with an empty bottle must not stand in the way of you and a perfect meal. Cooking involves loving yourself and the ones you cook for; it's about learning the fine art of creating something absolutely beautiful while at the trade, like parenthood.

My research on chicken tikka led me to its obvious cousin, tandoori chicken, and there is some obvious confusion about the two. The ingredients for the two are similar but only so much, tandoori chicken has more spices and is traditionally cooked in a tandoor (clay oven), while tikka is cooked on a traditional home or commercial grill. Needless to say, both can be made to perfection in an oven too.

Tandoori cooking originated in ancient Harappa and Mohenjo-Daro; tandoors dating back almost 2,500 years were unearthed in the area that sits in Pakistan today, but some believe that tandoori cooking originated in Rajasthan, India. Whichever discovery we choose to believe, the reality remains that the tandoor was the brainchild of the people from the subcontinent. Therefore we can readily claim the laurels of spreading tandoori cooking to all parts of the world.

Originally, meat was not cooked in Indian tandoors because it was difficult to achieve sufficient succulent tenderness. However with the process of meat tenderizing ingredients such as lemon juice, yogurt, raw papaya and raw pineapple, meat was introduced to the heat of the tandoor. Though it is to be noted that chicken and lamb were being made in the tandoor from the time of Mughal Emperor Jahangir, the ingredients were different from those in use today.

Ingredients

1 chicken (whole) with barbecue cuts (skin off)

½ cup yogurt

2 tsp red chilli powder (or to taste)

Salt to taste

3 tbsp lemon juice

¼ tsp black pepper powder

½ tsp ajwain, 1 tbsp. coriander seeds, 1 tsp cumin seeds (all roasted and ground)

½ tsp turmeric

½ tsp garam masala

1 tbsp fresh ginger garlic

¼ cup oil

Method

Mix all ingredients, rub marinade on chicken and let sit for 4 to 5 hours. Preheat oven to 400°F. Set chicken on rack of basting pan and bake, let the oil and juices drip on to the basting pan.

After 15 minutes, remove entire chicken and pan, pour collected juices and oil into a bowl and baste chicken.

Set chicken back in the oven, and baste chicken every 10 minutes for 30 minutes.

Once tender, set in platter, pour juices on chicken and serve with hot naan, sliced onions soaked in lemon juice or vinegar and a side of raita.

◆

BIHARI KABAB

Kabir-ul-Haq is from Bihar. He came to Pakistan with my Nani at the tender age of ten at the time of the great migration in 1947. Beeru, as we lovingly call him, was hired to play with the children. He has a strong Bihari accent, and makes the best Bihari kabab in the world.

Kabab, like all exotic South Asian foods, has an ancient history. It has travelled far and wide through time and regions, always evolving to suit the taste of the indigenous population and cities it passed through, adapting to local spices and cuisines, but maintaining its universal appeal through time. Undoubtedly, the most recognized Eastern food in the western part of the world, it has remained a favourite with desis, Middle Easterners, Arabs, Central Asians and Caucasians alike.

Kababs have always been a rustic favourite; and while they were said to be a prominent part of the Mughal menu, the variation of the modern day Bihari kabab is a purely Bihari and Bengali take on the kabab. And though Bihari kabab is made with meat chunks, much like the kababs in ancient times, it is nothing like the kababs that the Turks must have eaten. Instead it is the most delicious, melt-in-the-mouth meat chunk, infused with spices, yogurt and tenderizing papaya.

Ingredients
1 ½ kg veal chunk/beef chunk/boneless chicken/boneless mutton, thinly sliced and pounded
¾ cup yogurt
6 tbsp finely grated raw papaya with skin
¾ cup fried onions
4 tsp freshly grated ginger
4 tsp chopped garlic
1 tsp nutmeg powder
1 tsp cinnamon powder

1 ½ tsp cumin powder roasted
2 tsp paprika powder
2 tsp red chilli powder, or to taste
2 tsp poppy seeds
4 tsp Bihari kabab garam masala
¾ cup mustard oil (optional)
Salt to taste
(Mix in food processor and marinate meat)

Bihari kabab garam masala

(Use coffee grinder to make powder, and store unused portion in tightly sealed jar for future use)
2 tsp kabab chini
2 tsp fennel
2 star anise
4 tsp whole black peppercorns
2 cloves
½ nutmeg
1 tsp mace
10 green cardamom pods
6 black cardamom pods
2 tbsp coriander, whole
2 tbsp cumin seeds
12 dried red chillies

Method 1

Marinate meat for 24 hours, grill meat on skewers, set a coal to heat on the grill, drop oil on the coal and cover with metal lid (if available) to infuse meat with smoke of coal. Remove once meat is tender.

Method 2

Heat large pan with heavy base, pour a little oil and heat, set meat chunks on pan, cover and cook for 10 to 20 minutes, flip and cook for another 10 to 20 minutes. Transfer into an oven safe pan, broil for 10 to 15 minutes to dry moisture. Heat coal, sprinkle with oil and set in oven for a few minutes to infuse kababs with smoky coal. Serve with tamarind chutney, sliced onions, paratha or naan.

❧

Chapter 8

Punjab

The Land of Rivers, Rains and Oranges

Simla 1945

'Shireen it has been reported that you were seen with some boys last night? What do you have to say?' asked a very serious Mother Christina, Principal of the all-girls Convent of Jesus and Mary School, Simla.

'I would like to say that these claims are false. I retired at sunset last night and woke up at dawn today. You can ask my roommates, they will verify my habits,' responded a very confident Shireen. She was an expert at hoodwinking her superiors, and smooth at fabricating cover stories for her scandalous escapades. Whether it was stealing food from the school kitchen, shuffling test papers between classes, misplacing the school bell, or starting rumours for early dismissal, if a situation was amiss, Shireen was usually, lost to be found, within close proximity.

She usually managed to escape, and since she was a first-class student with a large fan-following amongst the student population, no one reneged on her. Her blossoming beauty and maturing body had become the talk of the school, everyone wanted to be her friend, and she basked in the attention. Sharmeena was her forever accomplice, but Shireen also needed temporary allies to move her fame train forward, and currently that train wreck was Hashmat Hakeem Sheikhani.

He was not a malicious boy, but certainly misled. His mother was a cook serving the Convent's nuns, hence his access to the school was permanent and effortless, and lately he had been providing spiked hookah to Shireen and her truant friends. The girls loved dipping their feet in clear and present danger—it was exciting, new and rebellious. However, Sharmeena was the voice of reason, the damper on the spirited expeditions of the young thrill-seekers, and lately opted out of all things involving Shireen and her new gang. Being in a gang encouraged mob mentality, that in essence was a recipe for trouble, and trouble made Sharmeena nervous.

It was Tuesday. Therefore pulao was on the menu, and halwa too. Shireen's Amma had sent pulao in a glistening tiffin box, and a large round earthen pot of hot halwa as dessert. The outside cafeteria bathed in an array of food aromas, the most effervescent being the one emanating from the fresh pulao. The benches were packed, as was the golden sunlight; bright, crisp and concentrated on the hungry group of girls sitting under the umbrella of the blue sky surrounded by a thicket of green.

Sharmeena was busy polishing off pulao when she saw Hashmat Hakeem Sheikhani gesturing across the field at Shireen, 'Why do you encourage him Shireen? He's foolish and trying to involve you in nefarious activities. This smoking of spiked hookah is unladylike, addictive, repulsive and so wrong. Why are you doing it? Is something bothering you?'

'You are too boring Sharmeena; this youth that we have, it is a one-time shot, and Hashmat is not dangerous. His mother is a disciple of Khawaja Gharib Nawaz, and he talks about visiting the

Ajmer Dargah. And I think anyone who is aiming to be dedicated to a Sufi saint can be trusted. And it's not like he's asking me to do anything indecent, is he? His only fault is that he is being a fun friend and sharing the hookah delights his father is pinching from Colonel Pritchett's house.'

'What? Colonel Pritchett smokes spiked hookah?' Sharmeena asked interested, suddenly having forgotten her reprimand of Shireen's antics.

'Not only that, Hashmat told me that he heard his parents talking about Mrs Pritchett's illicit affair with Mr Albert Field, the co-owner of Field's and Marshall's. Not that I blame Mrs Pritchett. Have you seen how old Colonel Pritchett is? Mrs Pritchett is a pretty young thing, and must have many unfulfilled desires.'

Sharmeena was perturbed at her friend's analysis of the entire event, but focused on the sweet carrot halwa, instead of trying to psychoanalyse Shireen. Amrita Kaur was eyeing the halwa from across the grounds too, and made her way to their table. She was Shireen's new friend and was angling to get a share of the orange delight. 'Legend, and my family story, has it that the Sikhs from Punjab introduced the carrot halwa to the house of the Mughals. The Emperors enjoyed its vibrant colour, flowery aroma, and slightly chewy texture, and it gained popularity far and wide spreading sweetness throughout the empire. So technically, since it was my ancestors who introduced carrot halwa to the world, I should be offered some,' said Amrita, and looking at her height and girth she appeared capable of devouring the entire feast.

'You big fat liar, you can't claim the origin of the carrot halwa ancestrally, and then gorge on my serving,' said Shireen laughing, protecting the halwa from Amrita's greedy eyes.

'Shireen, you claimed the pulao as your ancestral legacy, so why can't I claim the carrot halwa as mine? My grandfather, some centuries removed, was a cook in the royal kitchens of the Emperor Akbar, and sweet delicious carrot halwa is a result of his genius,' she said.

'Besides,' she added, 'the Mughal Empire was at its zenith, a dynasty that was splendid and modern and looking for trade with the rest of the world. The orange carrot had already spread far and wide to Europe, Middle East, and South Asia with the coming of the Dutch East India Company to the subcontinent in the seventeenth century. That's when my ancestor developed sweet carrot halwa in the kitchens of Akbar the Great.'

And there was truth to her alleged rendition. When the Mughal Empire began spreading and international traders brought in intriguing new goods for exchange, barter and purchase, the orange carrot is said to have been one such treasure. Carrots were originally purple in colour and indigenous to Afghanistan for almost 5,000 years. They came in colours such as red, yellow, black and white, but not orange, until the seventeenth century when the horticulturalists in the Netherlands decided to honour William of Orange, from the House of Orange, by creating an orange carrot. It could have been a coincidence, but in life there are no coincidences. The orange colour may have been a mutation of the red and yellow carrot with no significant link to the Royal House of Orange, but Dutch royalty claimed it, just because it had the power to do so at the time.

This new orange carrot was sweeter, prettier and of a non-sticky variety, making it popular amongst the cooks of the subcontinent, particularly Punjab. Vibrant Punjabis, much like the colour orange, liked the new imported carrot and the sweetness that came with it. And since it was an era when new cuisines were being developed by expert chefs and connoisseurs, the sweet imported carrot seemed to be of a perfect variety to be tried as the main ingredient in the halwa, with sweetness, milk and butter, sans the flour and nuts.

The province of Punjab took an instant liking to it, and developed innovative new recipes, sweet and savoury. It was a vegetable that peaked as a winter harvest and its abundance in glorious winters nudged the cooks to develop a hot delicious dessert best served any time of the day, before or after a meal, or as a side with chai.

Carrot halwa was an instant hit all over the Indian subcontinent, from pauper to prince; ranging from Hashmat Hakeem Sheikhani to the desperate descendants of Bahadur Shah Zafar.

∼

The orange tree was a magnificent array of hues in greens, yellows, reds and oranges. Shireen plucked two oranges from the fruit tree, and ate them, wiping the juice running down her neck with her dupatta scarf. She called out to Sharmeena who sat under the Banyan tree reading *Pride and Prejudice* by Jane Austen.

'Reading *Pride and Prejudice*, are you? Who's your favourite character?' Shireen asked, smacking her lips.

'I think I like Elizabeth. She's sensible, bright and an assertive girl, and with a good head on her shoulders, unlike you. Who do you like?'

'I like Mr Wickham, he's such a bad boy!'

'That's a first, I've never heard of anyone liking Mr Wickham. He's wicked and elopes with a fifteen-year-old girl. What is it that you like about him?'

'Don't hold that against him, he married her,' said Shireen, defending her decision to side with Mr Wickham.

'Okay, you can like him, that's your choice, let's not argue about it. Were you able to ask your mother for the pulao recipe? My family is having a lavish party this week in celebration of my brother's return from England. He got his law degree, and is going back to England to practice. Next week is the party, you are welcome to attend, as long as you share the recipe,' declared Sharmeena, hugging her friend.

'I'll come even if you don't invite me, and by the way I was joking about Mr Wickham. Who could like a philanderer such as him. I like Mr Bingley, he's so sweet.'

Sharmeena started laughing, 'I knew it. But you already have a Mr Bingley doting on you. What about your cousin Khusro? He worships the ground you walk on, and wants to marry you too? There, problem solved.'

The girls sat in the magical and lush Pinjore Gardens of Chandigarh, enjoying post-education recreation and pre-nuptial bliss. Fruit trees sprinkled the splendid leisure gardens constructed during the reign of Emperor Aurangzeb, and Shireen felt she was in a fruit orchard instead of a flower garden. The exotic fragrances of the flowers and the sweet-honeyed scent of the fruit attracted fluttering bees and unusually colourful birds. Shireen picked up an injured pigeon, limping in a flowerbed and nestled it close to her chest, stroking its smooth feathery surface. She almost felt compelled to lift it high and send it soaring, reminiscent of the grand gesture of Empress Nur Jehan, but showed restraint, nurturing the wounds of the bird instead.

Pondering her conversation with Sharmeena, she mulled the thought of Khusro's affections, he was a boring, predictable man, and too obvious about his fondness for her. Maybe she did like the reckless, adventurous kind, a mysterious lover waiting in the dark to sweep her off her feet. Shireen was willing to share the closely guarded family recipe of her mother's legendary pulao to meet him. And that's the barter she made with fate. Farhad Barani in exchange for pulao.

She had a feeling that he was around the dark corner and all she had to do was turn, and she did.

∽

Multan

Shireen loathed Multan as much as she loathed her life; it was hot and archaic, nothing like her majestic Simla. However, she loved the redemption of the city in the mosque culture, and the habshi halwa that was available year around. She could sit inside the Eidgah Mosque and eat halwa the entire length of the day, if only wishes were horses. If wishes were horses, her wish would be to move back to Simla, and not Karachi. The brand new capital city of Pakistan was her husband's next job posting, it was a city she knew nothing about, and was bored at the prospect of discovering.

The sound of thunder, clouds of dust, the revulsion caused by the sight of ever-present beggars, countless cemeteries with layers of bones, buried century after century since the sun had set on the Indus Valley Civilization, and the sweltering heat. The city might be historical, but it could never be magnificent, it could never be home. Shireen wanted to run to her mountain city, valley town, missionary education, to Sharmeena, and most of all to her Farhad. She stood in the centre of the ancient Hussain Agahi Bazaar. The market was dotted with tiny mosques, secret alleyways, smells of forgotten times, everything subcontinental—food, spices, sweat and people. Khusro revelled in the atmosphere of the central bazaar, but she was anesthetized about both him and his favourite jaunt.

The din in Hussain Agahi Bazaar reminded her of Sanjauli Market in Simla, and in a heartbeat she was sixteen again.

∽

Zohra looked at the remains of her mother, who looked asleep, but people all around her were crying, wailing, lamenting. Maybe she needed to do the same, and she did. Her older brother stood in the corner of the room, silent, motionless, alone. He kept asking, 'Why? Why did she have to die?' All four of his grandparents were still alive, but his mother was dead, it wasn't right.

Then came the realization, the tears, and sound of heartbreak. The room heard a wounded animal cry out in pain, it was Shireen's three children, the room remembered every moment of the moment, the disbelief, the emptiness, and the cries of 'Ammi' met with silence.

The three motherless children found themselves on the lost boat of life. Bracing the deep ocean, the relentless waves, anchorless and without destination. They were too young to understand that their mother had left them without imparting any valuable lesson, or saying goodbye.

There were no incredible morals taught.

No coaching in survival tips, or tutorials in success, failure or joyful experiences of life.

Regretfully, only tears.

And hunger. Hunger remained, separating the dead from the living. To satiate the gnawing craving in the belly, all attending Shireen's funeral decided to stay for the biryani and khichri made by Ma Khatija, since it was customary that neighbours, relatives and friends deliver food, for three days, to the house where a passing had occurred. The fire in the kitchen must not burn so that mourners get a chance to grieve the loss of the departed and not worry about cooking for themselves, or for visitors, at the time of a funeral.

While the body was fresh in the ground, the living had to eat to breathe, and to learn to live life without their loved one. That is just the way of the living.

Ma Khatija removed a tall stack of plates from the stocked sideboard in the dining room and distributed it amongst the occupants of the house. No one asked her why she was playing hostess. They all took her, a familiar face in the neighbourhood, for granted and let her serve them. Next she opened the heavy box of cutlery sitting atop the sideboard. It looked fancy and expensive, but she decided to use it nonetheless. She unwrapped the blue paper from around the silverware and counted twelve each of the dinner forks, dinner spoons, salad forks and teaspoons and distributed one each to the dinner guests, placing the six unused ones out of the forty-eight, back in the box. The cutlery set was kept with great care, hence it must have been expensive. She decided to wash all the used cutlery herself and put it back in the box before leaving for the night.

Ma Khatija made a large pot of khichri, hoping the three children of the deceased would eat it. She had never met Shireen, but only heard about her depression and obesity, and since the tragedy had occurred in her neighourhood she felt obligated to help the aggrieved family. Much later, after most of the people had left, Ma Khatija called the three children and fed them with her hands, telling them tales of the khichri.

'Khichri is another name for wholesome goodness and one more commonality, amongst many, that connects subcontinental households across borders, languages and ethnicities; needless to say, mothers and aunties absolutely love feeding their families khichri, like I am feeding you now. The origin of khichri is a few millennia old, and it belongs to our land as much as its soil. Conquerors, discoverers and imperialists came from around the world, were fed a meal of the local khichri and fell in love with it. Babies and children in the family are nourished with khichri and grandparents are cherished on it. A long time ago, when the

Mughal Emperor Humayun was in exile in Persia he entertained Persian Princes with khichri, and they loved the flavour of this rustic delight.'

'Ma Khatija can you tell us more stories?' asked Zohra, wide eyed and innocent while merrily accepting each mouthful of kindly fed khichri. 'One day Emperor Jahangir, son of Akbar the Great was riding through the rich and vibrant land of Gujarat, night was falling and the Emperor's entourage needed to rest for the night. The Emperor was served khichri by a local chef. It was made with millet instead of rice. Emperor Jahangir relished the taste, and decided to take the Gujarati chef, who had prepared the delight, with him to be employed in the royal kitchens of the Mughals.'

'Are you from Gujarat, Ma Khatija?'

'Yes, I am, and that's why I know this story so well. Khichri is said to be the ultimate Ayurvedic detox food, packed with flavour, health, and nourishment for the body and soul. Rice and lentils cooked together are said to be the ideal comfort food and have been around for thousands of years. So Zohra, the next time someone asks you about a perfect food, tell them to eat khichri.'

'Tell me more, tell me more,' said little Salma excitedly.

'Here we go girls. Let me tell you the journey of khichri to kedgeree,' said Ma Khatija. 'It is our very own khichri that was christened kedgeree by the British. They added boiled eggs and fish to it, doing away with the essential dal altogether. The Anglo Indians served khichri made with rice and dal for breakfast, with freshly caught fish. Once transported to the British Isles, the aristocracy in Britain, started serving kedgeree for breakfast during their country-house getaways. And so the wholesome khichri has passed the test of time, regions and classes and remains that one dish which is still enjoyed best when made with its original ingredients. Needless to say, there are countless versions and recipes of the hearty khichri, but my favourite is still the original. And that's the one I made for you children today.'

Ma Khatija fed the three children simple goodness for the sake of simple goodness, and nothing else.

The two girls looked animated and involved with the motherly neighbour, but not Farhad, he was torn between apathy and frenzy. He sat with his two younger sisters bracing for a firestorm of emotion to follow the tears, but nothing came except sadness. Zohra hugged her brother, and henceforth grew up thinking he was her saviour. As for Farhad, he became a parent to his two younger siblings, paying heavily for the sins of his father, and mother too.

Nights changed to years, years to decades, and eventually came melancholy. The tragic reality of Farhad's melancholia was reflected in the overwhelming truth of the void his mother Shireen had left behind, and the pensive side of the despondence came from days of reflection, acceptance, and the realization of life and its unexplainable mechanisms. Farhad began to understand his part in the sagacious and meticulous framework of life. There was always a plan, a strategy much beyond his understanding.

And then one day he decided never to return to Shireen's graveside. His resolute decision to move away from her gravestone, and the unceremonious walk from the cemetery, held the greatest meaning. It was an odyssey, only because he understood it, for himself and for his mother. The walk implied that however incredible, or meaningless the journey or the companion, life was all about letting go. He let go of his mother and the land she was buried in, for good.

He became an immigrant, and each journey home to Pakistan became revered. It grew synonymous with a journey within, almost like it held religious significance akin to Haj or Yatra, bringing with it the wisdom that a philosophic journey is only understood if coupled with a laborious physical journey, a walk, a mountain climb, or a journey across seas. The realization helped him heal, helped him forgive, helped him let go of what could not be controlled, helped him accept what was, helped him embrace the promise of tomorrow, and, most importantly, it helped him understand that one must not dwell on memories but revel in them. He empathized with people who had yet to suffer the pain of losing a mother, and acknowledged the truth that the suffering and the final goodbye was a tireless journey within, as old as the dust we return to, and inescapable.

Henceforth, whenever he travelled, the seat next to him was vacant. Initially he did not notice it, but it became too much of a coincidence to escape his attention. He interpreted that his mother accompanied him everywhere he went; he chose to walk away from her, but she never let go of him.

He never forgave her for packing on excess weight, he never forgave sugar for always finding its way into the kitchen, and he never understood what drove his mother to unhappiness. She was beautiful once. Farhad finally found his peace in not having all the answers. He found his answer in the journey he took often, with an empty seat next to him. At the end of the journey there was no mother to greet him, or to answer his questions, but the journey was not about greetings, it was about finding that elusive thing called peace.

KHICHRI

Khichri, another name for wholesome goodness and one more commonality, amongst many, that connects subcontinental households across borders, languages and ethnicities; needless to say, desi mothers absolutely love feeding their families khichri. They love its basic cooking technique and the perfect sustenance it provides for the entire family. My mother served khichri with a side of raita, kachumber and shami kababs, it truly was one of our most favoured lunch or dinner menus.

It is the ultimate Ayurvedic detox food, packed with flavour, health, and nourishment for the body and soul. Rice and legumes/lentils cooked together are a perfect union of amino acids essential for our bodies; it is said to be the perfect protein and has been around for thousands of years.

Ingredients
½ cup moong dal
1 cup rice
3 to 4 cups water, or as required
¼ tsp cumin seeds
3 to 4 bay leaves
3 to 4 cloves
Salt to taste

Method
Wash and soak rice and dal separately for a couple of hours. Rinse thoroughly and set aside.

Take 3 to 4 tbsp of oil or ghee and fry bay leaves and cloves for a few seconds, then add dal and rice to the pot and fry for 8 to 10 minutes.

Add water to the pot and let sit on medium heat, cover and cook, bringing the heat to low and letting (covered) cook until dal and rice is tender, adding more water if required.

If you want to add vegetables (spinach, tomato, cauliflower, peas or any other vegetable of choice), these can be added when the khichri is three-fourths done, and then cooked to completion and tenderness.

Sprinkle cumin seeds and onion bhagaar if desired, serve individually or with a side of raita, salad and shami kabab.

◆

GAJAR KA HALWA

Delightfully delicious—that's the only way to describe gajar ka halwa. Who thought of adding sugar, milk and ghee to grated carrots, simmering the mix until the milk dried, and serving it up as a delectable dessert? Legend has it that the Sikhs from Punjab introduced it to the house of the Mughals.

The shared food heritage between Pakistan and India is fascinating, we share the same food stories and love the same foods and can rightfully both lay claim to all foods as our own. This not only makes for a delightfully interesting dinner conversation with friends, but also makes for a common ground to share family recipes and stories.

Ingredients
2 ¼ lb carrots (orange)
1.60 to 1.80 litres of milk
½ pint half-and-half (a mix of equal amounts of whole milk [not skimmed milk] and light cream)
⅓ pint heavy whipping cream
1 ¾ cups sugar
2 to 3 tbsp butter (unsalted)
¼ cup oil
8 to 10 cardamom pods
1 tbsp raisins
2 tbsp blanched and chopped almonds

and grate carrots and set aside. Bring milk to boil and add ...ilk and carrot mixture come to boil then add half-and-...r, stirring constantly. Keep stirring until mixture comes to boil, reducing heat to medium. Once milk evaporates (should take 1 ½ to 2 hours) add heavy cream, stirring constantly. Once cream evaporates add butter, oil and cardamom stirring contantly, keeping the flame medium to high. Keep stirring until oil separates, and the colour is a rich beautiful deep orange. Garnish with raisins and almonds and serve.

◆

SARSOON KA SAAG

Nothing has more flavour than a mother's love, but the only thing that comes close to it is the smell of the land, more uniquely 'mera aur tera gaon' (our village), the one we all originate from, the one our forefathers left behind when they moved for greener pastures from those glorious green pastures. I believe all our gastronomical experiences and the sensory emotions they evoke are a reflection of our childhood experiences, and my first memory of the endless fields of yellow flowers (sarsoon kay khet or fields of mustard), is unadulterated childlike awe. We were driving from Karachi to Rawalpindi through Tarinda, a village in Punjab, when I saw an impressive black bull standing in a field of gold, a black crow perched atop his head. I vividly remember exclaiming, 'black gorilla and black crow standing inside yellow flowers', I was three, life was full of possibilities and my first meal of sarsoon ka saag and makkai ki roti was just around the corner.

Nothing is more quintessentially Punjab than sarsoon ka saag and makkai ki roti, it's an earthy hearty food, abundant in flavour, nutrients, simplicity and colour; much like the land and the people it belongs to. Sarsoon has been indigenous to the foothills of the Himalayas for over five millennia. Now imagine endless fields of yellow, the colour of the sarsoon flowers, at the feet of the magnificent Himalayas and the sturdy mountain folk who have been enjoying the creaminess of sarsoon forever! Sarsoon is winter and spring fare and its seasonal abundance in Punjab, both sides of the Wagah, makes it a Punjabi favourite for rustics and urbanites alike.

It is a vegetarian delight made from the leaves of the mustard plant, the same plant that gives us the delicious condiment, mustard. The desi mustard green, grown in Pakistan and India is a smooth flat textured leaf, but another variety includes a crumpled frilly leaf, spunky in look but earthy in taste.

Historically, sarsoon ka saag, was generally the rural people's food in Punjab, and the robust homemade butter-topped saag fit the hardworking lifestyle of the village people laboriously working the agricultural lands of the fertile province. They almost always justified and propagated the consumption of desi ghee (clarified butter), desi makhan (butter), Lassi (yogurt drink), desi paneer (cottage cheese) and chaach (buttermilk), and this practice has since carried to urban Punjab. A rich cuisine it may be, but its pure, farm fresh and organic composition makes it a winner in the world of engineered and preservative laden food.

Sarsoon ka saag and makkai ki roti is down-home rustica and its nutritious content and the winter harvest is why mothers feed it to their children. Mothers know best. For generations they have been cooking this Punjabi favourite, and for good reason.

Traditionally, the real sarsoon ka saag is cooked sans masala, just a dash of salt and ginger, mixed in with the greens; mustard greens, green chillies, spinach, and bathua (pigweed) or methi (fenugreek). And the real cooks, our mothers and grandmothers, who follow the age-old family recipe without the modern touch to suit the contemporary lifestyle still cook it the same way. It was said to be slow-cooked and hand stirred, an entirely different style of cooking. Sarsoon has an almost pungent taste to it and is therefore cooked in the company of other greens like broccoli, radish, spinach, pigweed, fenugeek and at times turnip. So when the time came for me to make sarsoon ka saag and makkai ki roti, I turned to none other than Dadi. She has been making saag for our clan for more than fifty years, and proudly and rightly claims that the lesser the number of ingredients the better it is. The recipe is her mother-in-law's who lived in Rupnagar, pre-Partition India, and, in turn, had learnt to cook the real Punjabi saag from her own mother-in-law. I can, therefore, rightfully claim that it is a family recipe going back to the later part of the nineteenth century.

Ingredients (Sarsoon ka Saag)

4 lb mustard greens (chopped with stem)
2 lb spinach
2 lb pigweed (if available)
½ cup water
1 tsp brown sugar or 1 tsp jaggery (secret ingredient)
5 to 7 serrano peppers
Salt to taste
1 inch piece of ginger
2 tbsp corn flour dissolved in ¼ cup water
2 large sliced onions and 1 tsp chopped garlic (fried in ¼ cup oil for garnish)
Dollop of butter per serving, if desired

Method

Pour ½ cup water and mustard greens in a large pot and cover and simmer for 15 to 20 minutes. Add spinach, salt, sugar, peppers, ginger and pigweed (if available) and cook for another 15 to 20 minutes. Put in a blender to roughly blend, add dissolved cornflour and cook for a few minutes. Garnish and serve.

Ingredients (Makkai ki Roti; makes 12 to 14)

4 cups corn flour
2 ½ to 3 cups warm water
4 tbsp chopped cilantro (optional)
2 finely chopped serrano peppers (optional)
Salt, if desired
Oil, as needed

Method

Add warm water to flour, knead dough adding cilantro and pepper. Make balls and flatten to roti on parchment paper. Heat pan with a teaspoon of oil and transfer roti with parchment paper, remove paper and flip roti. Cook 2 to 3 minutes on each side until golden. Serve hot with a dollop of butter.

❧

Chapter 9

Ramazan

The Month of Abstinence and the Ring

Any indulgence that requires abstinence through physical denial to further illuminate philosophic clarity and emotional balance has to be a delightfully enjoyable pleasure, and food happens to maintain an elite status as one such delight. The yearly arrival of Ramazan, the holy month of fasting, is a certainty. However, what is not is the maintenance of a gleeful temperament throughout the month.

The month begins with utmost fervour, but the enthusiasm starts waning as does the full moon after the middle of the month, and the sighting of the crescent, announcing the end of a month of fasting becomes a priority on the night of the twenty-ninth of Ramazan.

Will the sliver in the sky appear for all to welcome Eid the following day, or will there be one more day of fasting? Certainly a crucial *to be or not to be*, almost as significant as Prince Hamlet's dilemma in William Shakespeare's *Hamlet*.

Muslims around the world go into a preparation frenzy as households focus on the traditional month-long Ramazan schedule: Special foods to be eaten at Sehri before daybreak, and as the sun sets at Iftar time; shorter work days, special Taraweeh prayer at mosques, and mostly, abstinence from all things delicious, wrong and pleasurable while the sun is in the skies.

The month is considered the holiest in the Muslim calendar, and by the time it departs it has taught valuable lessons pertaining to life, and an improved way of living it; gratitude for what we possess, empathy for the hungry, and a temporary dose of restraint in demanding instant gratification.

Consequently, these lessons solidify the truth that introspective awareness of the metaphysical ensues after a test of physical endurance and mental discipline. In essence, acceptance of physical suffering through abstinence in feast, elevates the process of self-reflection and contemplation. Further, initiating a profound understanding of the code of conduct, ethics, values and the dispassionate realization that the greatest pleasures in life are to be enjoyed within a framework of balance, moderation and legitimacy. And this awareness is what determines man's status as the most evolved of God's creations.

Today is the first day of fasting, and sitting in my rocking chair, undernourished, I think of all the right reasons for denying my body food and water until sundown, and I come up with plenty. This is unlike my younger self when I could come up with absolutely nothing, except my promise of staying true to the morning pledge of maintaining hunger and thirst until sundown. However, as an adult I see wisdom in my childish rationale for holding on to a promise. It's the respect of that very promise: indoctrinating in the mind of the thinker the true value in self-control and abstinence from the greatest pleasures of life until the time is right.

Invariably my hungry mind shifts focus to sounds of our kitchen, and that of the neighbours, prepping the Iftar and dinner spread for the evening. The sounds soon change to delicious aromas of fritters, pakoray, samosay, chana chaat, fruit chaat and dahi baray, putting my ravenous insides in turmoil, and before losing my mind to the same, I call out to Leo. The nine-month-old puppy bounces off the floor onto my lap, looking for love and finding it in the right curves. I toss a stale biscuit across the verandah coaxing a fetch. The hardened biscuit slides under the cane sofa through the little opening between the base of the sofa and the floor, and as Leo struggles to grab the treat from under the sofa he pulls out his old play pal, the lost hot pink duster. Taken aback at his misplaced find he pauses for a second, smells it, loses interest, fetches the biscuit and comes running to me, and together we walk to the dining room as I get ready to break my fast to the sound of prayer.

～

The dining table features an array of delights in feast, and festivities in sound. Dadi, Abbu and Ammi break their fast in keeping with the traditional practice of biting into a date, while I tear into a crunchy pakora. I don't know if it's the sound of the crispy crunch that brings a smile, the years of happy memories that come with the joys of pakora-eating come Iftar time, or just the arrival of Ramazan in spring. Whatever it may be, I find myself blissfully comfortable, the smell of the homemade samosa takes me to my childhood and school. Anyone who attended a missionary school in Karachi has to have tasted the legendary potato samosa sold at the tuck shop. All the tuck shops owned by Mr Bonanza, therefore carried the same golden brown, crispy, flaky, delicious samosa, and at forty-paisa a pop, it was a real delight to chow down during the twenty-minute lunch break.

And if the school samosa wasn't delicious enough to pack on weight, our chowkidar used to make the best home-made samosay. Hence, samosa is an active partner to biscuits for the weight crimes committed against me.

'Hey Dadi, does the samosa really belong to the subcontinent?'

'No, it does not. It migrated from Central Asia and is an immigrant food on a desi plate, but needless to say, it has adjusted splendidly well to its adoptive land, and has actually become one of us. The immigrant samosa travelled the length and breadth of the region and came to the subcontinent along ancient trade routes of Central Asia. It was actually a traveller's snack and used to be called Samsa, named after the Pyramids of Central Asia.'

'Why haven't you told me this before, and how do you know this, Dadi?'

'One must learn all they can about their ancestry, and since your academically inclined Dada dedicated much of his free time to researching the bloodline and the historical social studies associated with it, I absorbed a lot of information too,' she replies.

'I think it was your Dada's way of trying to impress and charm me,' she says laughing, and then continues, 'It is said that the snack became such an intrinsic and favoured menu item in the royal kitchens of the fourteenth-century dynasty of Muhammad Tughlaq, that he often requested for them to be made with onions, ghee and meat.'

She helps herself to a samosa and continues, 'The poet Amir Khusro wrote that Delhi royalty enjoyed the snack immensely, and apparently that tradition continues today. From Delhi to Lahore and Karachi to Bombay, the subcontinent is a fan of the samosa. The great ancient traveller Ibn Battuta has written that the samosa was served as a delightful appetizer at the dinner table of the Tughlaqs before the third course of pulao. And the Mughals were great connoisseur of the delight too.'

'Pulao, appears to be a favourite amongst royalty and peasantry, alike!' I declare emphatically as Jalal walks in with an almost royal platter of mutton pulao. I find myself taking a deep breath to soak in the effervescence of plumped rice and lovingly make myself a delicious serving of pulao with a side of beetroot yogurt and vinegar-soaked onion, and say a prayer for the ancestors who may have enjoyed the same delight.

Glancing at my plate, which appears well-proportioned and in keeping with the mantra of balance in Ramazan, I summon silence to accompany my feast in nirvana, but it escapes me. And suddenly I feel an insatiable desire for a luxuriant slice of luscious chocolate cake, delicious, sublime and a perfect dessert to feast on in the spring of life.

The unexplained dilemma must remain,
The cravings are similar, the pleasure the same,
The delicate choices we make determine our fate,
Desires are many, licit charms we must create.

~

With Ramazan and Eid season upon us, Musings Over a Cup of Tea has been busy as a bee, more so than B. Bees. Of course that is farthest from the truth, but who's counting. Our office space is in the up and coming Zamzama Commercial Area, and with Eid holidays almost around no one is in the mood to work, but I'm here at the office trying to clean my desk and get organized for a return following the holidays.

It's been almost three months since I last met Faiz, and his absence and the unsaid is now starting to chip at my spunk, but not enough to affect my creativity. At least not yet!

His involvement in the Ghazi Barotha Hydroelectric Power Project has temporarily placed him some nine-hundred and fifty miles from Karachi, on the Indus River in northwest Pakistan, near Tarbela Dam. The massive engineering undertaking is a joint venture between five engineering firms—two local, two of British origin and one American firm, while the construction contractors are headed by people from Italy and China. It's a colossal project presumed to wrap up by the beginning of the next century, and is expected to lower power-generation costs, positively impacting the infrastructure of Pakistan in the long run.

With his hands full, designing towering feats in real life, I must hardly be a priority. Faiz's understated interest has remained even keeled, just enough to keep my hopes afloat, but not enough to pin my hopes on. Agitated, I reach for the jar of biscuits on my desk, but restrain myself. Even if I'm not fasting this week it's best to practice abstinence. Practice does make perfect.

'Are you not fasting?' I look up to see him standing in the open doorway, leaning into the doorframe with his arms folded across his chest. Smiling, charming and casual, and in no rush to come into the office, I lean into my chair soaking in the adrenaline rush, aware of a nerve ticking in my head and thinking, *he's back, and he's here.* Maintaining a somewhat calm persona and smiling, I raise an eyebrow giving a sassy response.

'I am.'

'Liar.'

'Why would you think I am lying?' I ask, smiling sheepishly.

'I don't know, you tell me?' He asks, grinning widely.

'I'll tell you, but then I'll have to marry you.'

His unabashed laughter is loud and has me laughing uncontrollably too, and in an instance I feel tension and stress releasing itself through a moment of shared intimacy. His rather trendy iris purple cotton shirt rolled to the elbows, and tucked into navy blue corduroy pants, adds pep to the room. 'How long have you been standing there, and when did you get back to Karachi?'

'Long enough, and this morning. How have you been?' he asks, eyes smiling and walking into the room, taking a seat opposite my desk. After exchanging formalities, informally, we catch up on the events of the last few months. He tells me about his recent visit to Lahore, and I can't help but wonder if he encountered the hot pink girl from Haveli Niazbagh. And in that moment as Faiz keeps talking about his project I get wistful, thinking of all the possibilities of us playing hide and seek with the obvious. I remind myself that there is nothing obvious about the path both of us have taken. Except for a couple of phone calls by a mysterious lady a few months ago, there is no indication of anything or anyone going anywhere.

Or is there?

And in an instant I lose a little bit of my spunk. I cue the child in me, and she directs me to get a glass of water to save face. Maintaining my calm and nodding to whatever is being said I walk to the filing cabinet, silently pouring myself water in a large twenty-ounce mug, pulling my loose hair into a bun and securing it in place with a pen, and then walk back to my chair.

There is silence in the room and Faiz is now sitting at the edge of my desk, on my side a couple of feet away, 'Why are you nodding still? I stopped talking a few minutes ago.'

'Oh, I was silently talking to myself. What made you think I was nodding to whatever you were saying?' I say, taking on the pose of a sleuth while sipping my water.

'Have you been to Tarbela Dam?'

'I have once, maybe ten years ago.'

'Come with me next time I go?'

'Are you asking me to run away with you?' I can't resist asking and start laughing before he can react to my question.

'Am I?' he asks, in a half standing position with his arms folded and legs crossed, looking at me as if gauging my response to his almost rhetorical question.

And in an instant his face is an inch away from mine. I can

smell his cologne and so much more. Holding onto the arms of my chair he maintains his balance playfully rubbing his nose with mine, stalling for a moment, and then gently pulls away.

It is impossible to think, and capture this moment in time, simultaneously. And dawns the awareness that subtle intimacy and romance do not require much practice; much like animals, humans are naturally inclined to react to positive chemistry when the variables are right. I wait for a response from him. Faiz appears unfrazzled, and softly says, 'I am.'

'I am what?' I ask, somehow managing to speak coherently.

'I am asking you to run away with me,' he repeats calmly.

'Am I allowed to bring something along?'

'No, you are not!'

'Why not?'

He pulls me off the chair, gently removes the pen from my hair and letting it loose, says softly, 'You talk too much.'

'I know,' I reply winking.

He casually picks up my glass of water and drinks its entire contents. The familiarity, and intimacy of the gesture catch me off guard and I find myself taken aback. Sensing it he says the obvious without addressing the unsaid, 'I was travelling this morning, and therefore am not fasting.' And then winking he says, 'I'll be fasting tomorrow, so don't come looking for me.'

'Worry about yourself, I've been famously known to resist the irresistible!'

Chuckling he says, 'Glad to know it, Ayesha. That's my girl.'

⌇

The duality of food is a concept mostly misunderstood. There is a very joyous, and a very dark side to it. Too much of it is gluttony, too little results in starvation. Eating to fill emotional needs leads to dependence, sadness and elation, while fad eating is a marketing menace which coaxes an unhealthy courtship. And once fad eating has enslaved its victims it takes the role of Dr Frankenstein's monster, haunting its victims to stay within the guidelines set by the money-driven businesses promoting fad dieting.

The delightful side on the other hand is one of the greatest blessings gifted to us: eating in moderation, savouring every bite, sharing it as a community, exchanging cuisines and recipes, travelling with it, and most importantly celebrating with it.

My relationship with food is passionate. It never abandons me and is always willing to please in indulgent ways. However, it is a one-sided love affair. I have only used it for my own gain, never understanding its role in my life until it was denied to me, but clearly it has been denied to me before. What changed this time around, I ask myself?

Maybe the answer is elsewhere. My newfound knowledge about Nani's circumstances, and the tragedy of her young death, and my repeated conversations with Dadi with respect to life and food, and her latest perspective on it, 'Have you ever thought about food as a lover?'

'Seriously Dadi, you really want to have this conversation with me?' I ask, almost cheekily.

'Yes, I do. Food is a necessity, a pleasure and a nurturing force, but all we do is take from it. Imagine, if we were to treat a lover in the same manner, what would he do? Starvation is like denying a lover, gluttony is hedonistic, fad dieting is the unwillingness to accept your lover as a whole, and emotional eating is almost akin to turning to a lover in times of crises, or extreme elation. Where is the conventional in all this, the average, or the normal in the relationship?

'For food to treat you right, you have to treat it right too, reciprocate the love it shows you by maintaining a balance and consistency, and slipping occasionally. Learn to manage it, recognize its flaws, accept it wholeheartedly, and then judge how it treats you. Don't be dismissive of it. It's natural sustenance knows your body better than you do, and has been around far longer than you and I. Relish it, and let it relish you.'

Dadi's perspective is almost meditative, but its application is harder than dictated. Regardless, it's refreshing and makes practical and reflective sense, therefore worth a try. With that thought reigning, I head to the kitchen to try a small serving of sheer khurma, the quintessential meethi Eid dessert, and also to sneak a peek at the feast being prepared for the chai trolley for Eid festivities.

The appearance of the crescent in the skies promises the arrival of Eid, and the *dark knight*. Reiterating my belief that the best promises are made over a delicious cup of chai and a trolley, and the best chai is served in the land of the River Indus.

~

Eid, the official day of feasting is here, and the eating begins from the break of dawn until the wee hours of the morning, and for three days straight, no exaggeration. After twenty-nine days of a gruelling schedule of eating and starving, to stuffing my face with food, come Iftar time, my body and mind are ready to welcome normal eating, and appreciate eating anytime too. So here I am enjoying a small portion of sheer khurma and momentary solitude sitting in my rocking chair.

The annual Eid lunch gluttony, expectedly, plays the role of sedative and all have retired to their chambers for a leisurely late-afternoon siesta. The lunch, hosted by my parents, is delightful every year. The laughter is loud, cousins many, friends aplenty, gossip in abundance and the food traditionally subcontinental.

The lavish spread is prepared in our kitchen, and Dadi and Ammi take pride in playing the perfect hostesses. From the menu, to the fresh flower décor, cutlery, crockery and distribution of Eidi (cash gifts distributed on Eid), the arrangement is perfect, and if the other occupants of the household complain about the both of them being fussy about the Eid lunch, they exclaim, and usually in unison, 'It's Eid *thevaar*, the blessed festival of Eid, we think it deserves to be fussed over.'

This year Ajit's family sent a large platter of homemade besan laddu, which was a raging hit. The crumbly textured sweetness left me wanting to inhale an entire helping, but Dadi's wisdom kept reverberating, and I made a sensible choice with regard to portion, in keeping with my newfound relationship with food.

The white and yellow roses flanking the red platter, playing host to the besan delight, makes an inviting picture, and I grab my markers to make a quick sketch. Halfway through I doze off on Dadi's daybed, waking to the sound of the late evening call to prayer. My mind still dazed from sleep I wake up to the sound of the gate closing and footsteps in my verandah.

'Wake up sleepyhead,' exclaims Sofia.

'Hey, that was an unusually quiet entrance. Why didn't you come for lunch?'

'I told you I had to go to my grandparents. Anyways let's have chai in the garden. It's too gorgeous an evening to be sitting under a roof.'

Grabbing my sketchpad and markers I follow Sofia to the garden.

Once comfortable in the garden chairs, Sofia garbs my sketchpad and starts sketching my hand. It's not the prettiest rendition of my hand, but it's a rendition nonetheless, 'Why are you doodling on my hand, and that too so imperfectly? I think this sketch belongs in the garbage bin. You just concentrate your mind on writing, let me take care of the artwork.'

'It's lovely, you just don't have eyes to appreciate real art, yet!'

∼

'What are you doing with my sketchbook, Faiz?'

'Just a minute,' he says picking up a red sketching marker and drawing something on the pad, and casually hands it back to me.

The sketch Sofia drew of my hand is now wearing a ring on its fourth finger. I think I'm keeping this sketch, it seems it belongs to me.

∼

PAKORAY

Ramazan, rain, summer vacation and pakoray, and this is where I break into the popular song, 'My Favourite Things', from the movie *Sound of Music*. Yes, pakoray and Ramazan go hand in hand, as do rain and Pakoray. Ammi always had a pakora platter ready come Maghrib in Ramazan, and since us fussy siblings did not appreciate the vegetable pakora platter until much later in life, she would make sliced boiled-egg pakoras for us, and a delightful Iftar they made.

If you grew up in Pakistan or North India you obviously know what a pakora is, [in South India it goes by a different name]; it is the quintessential desi snack found in every street corner and home. Come Ramazan, winter or monsoon. Pakora is a popular street food, but in a desi household pakora is very much a homemade food item as well. In many Punjabi homes pakoray and rain go together, like in Lucknow, pakoray and teatime.

History tells us that spring was the time when the locals enjoyed eating fried pakoray, kachorian, purian, all kinds of batter-fried or fried foods, and thus they decided to dip vegetables in batter and fry them in the spring and monsoon season to celebrate these seasons. It became a street food, affordable, quick and scrumptious, and in being so also developed into being a sumptuous snack to be taken pleasure in at Iftar time. When breaking fast, desis of the subcontinent have trained their taste buds to savour fried delicacies, hence pakora is a must-have Iftar treat, almost as much as the khajoor (date). Come Ramazan or not, my household remains in a constant state of Pakora- frenzy. Here it is from my kitchen to yours.

Ingredients

2 cup gram flour
2 green chillies, chopped
2 medium-sized potatoes, sliced
2 to 3 boiled eggs, sliced
1 small eggplant, sliced
Spinach leaves
6 tbsp chopped cilantro
Salt to taste
Red chilli powder to taste
1 tsp ajwain
1 tsp coriander seeds
1 tsp cumin seeds (pan roasted and roughly ground)
1 tsp baking powder (level)

Method

Mix ingredients, eyeballing amount of water and deep fry until crisp and crunchy. Enjoy with chaat masala, yogurt, chutney or ketchup.

Note: Use any vegetable of preference to make pakoray.

◆

SAMOSA

How is one to capture the essence of a samosa through the written word? One has to smell it, taste it and savour it to really appreciate it. Yes, that's the only way to really experience a samosa.

In Spanish, a similar kind of pastry is called empanada; it tastes like the stepbrother of the samosa, but almost touches the same taste buds.

Ingredients

2 cups flour
4 tbsp oil
12 to 14 tbsp water
1 tsp carom seeds
Salt to taste
Oil for frying

Potato stuffing Boil 3 medium-sized potatoes. Once boiled, peel, add salt to taste, ½ tsp cumin, ¼ tsp red chilli powder, 1 tsp chopped cilantro, ¼ tsp chopped green chillies, fried onions, ½ tsp carom seeds, and ½ tsp crushed coriander seeds. Mash together and fry on high heat in 4 tbsp oil for a few minutes.

Keema stuffing: Brown ½ medium-sized onion in 2 to 3 tbsp oil. Once golden brown, add 1 lb ground meat, ½ tsp cumin, ½ tsp red chilli powder, ½ tsp garam masala, ½ tsp ginger and garlic paste and salt to taste. Cook on medium heat for 15 to 20 minutes, raising the heat to high and stirring constantly for another 5 minutes or until the oil separates from the meat.

Method

Mix all ingredients for shell, knead for 10 minutes forming dough, cover with damp cloth and set aside for an hour in room temperature. Then divide into 6 equal balls of dough, flatten them into 6 round rotis, cut each in half making a semicircle.

On the straight edge of the sliced roti apply some water and fold to form a seal. Stuff the prepared samosa cone with the potato, or mince stuffing, apply water on the round cone circumference and pinch edges to seal.

Slide samosa into hot oil (at full heat), turning heat to low after sliding it in and until it turns golden brown. Increase heat again and remove from fryer. Drain and enjoy.

◆

SHEER KHURMA

Eid-ul-Fitr is the most wonderful time of the year and the memories associated with Ramazan and meethi Eid are joyous, filled with sweetness, good times, Eidi, family, friends and sheer khurma. I was never a sheer khurma or saviyaan (vermicelli) fan, up until my mother asked me how any foodies could say they did not like sheer khurma, and my response was, 'I've never tasted it, I just don't like the way it looks.' My mother gave me an exasperated look and introduced me to sheer khurma, and I became a fan for life.

My mother made the most delicious sheer khurma every year, as must have yours, and the Sheer was as warm as mother's embrace and as sweet as her love. Returning home from Eid namaz, my father would enter through the front door where we would line up for our Eidi, and our wonderful cook Jalal would pull in the trolley laden with delectable Eid treats, and there was the sheer khurma, sitting pretty and delicious, front and centre.

Sheer khurma literally means milk and dates, sheer means milk in

Persian and khurma means dates, and how and when vermicelli was added to this delightful dessert, your guess is as good as mine. It is believed that, since Saudi Arabia abounds with the harvest of dates people would break their fast with dates, as we still do today, and feast on a milk and date dessert come Eid morning. Hence, sheer khurma is a Eid-ul-Fitr delight in all Muslim households.

This simple yet delicious sweet dish is versatile as it can be served hot or cold. Dates one of the main ingredients (since in those days this milk and date dessert was sweetened with dates and not sugar) that enhance this delicacy, are in themselves nutritious and a complete meal, like milk. Generally fresh ripened dates are used in the making of sheer khurma, but many use dry dates also.

The Eid fiesta brings with it sublime food flavours. After a month of strict abstinence, Eid-ul-Fitr is most associated with feasting and would not be complete without the sheer khurma and its abundance. It is delicious, quick and makes for a sweet Eid morning.

Ingredients

8 cups or 2 kg full cream milk
100 grams vermicelli
4 oz condensed milk
8 oz sugar
10 to 12 green cardamom pods
10 to 12 dates (chopped lengthwise)
½ cup (pistachios, almonds, cashews, raisins)
Pinch of salt

Method

Bring milk to boil, add vermicelli and keep stirring, simmer for 15 to 20 minutes, adding sugar, condensed milk, cardamom, salt and dates. Let simmer for 20 minutes to half hour, reducing the quantity.

Add dry fruit, cook for a few more minutes. Pour into serving bowl, garnish and serve hot or cold.

◆

BESAN LADDU

Ingredients (makes 18 to 20)
5 ¼ cups besan
2 ½ cups ghee
½ cup whole milk
2 cups castor sugar
15 to 20 green cardamom pods crushed, or green cardamom powder
15 to 20 almonds to garnish

Method
Put ghee and besan in a pot and cook for 10 minutes, stirring constantly, at a medium to low heat. Then, add milk and cook for another 10 minutes. Turn off the heat, add sugar and green cardamom, and mix well.

Cool the mixture to room temperature and form round balls. Garnish with crushed almonds before serving.

Store in an airtight container at room temperature for up to 20 days. If the weather is very hot, store in the fridge and heat before serving.

◆

Chapter 10

Baraat

Sounds of a Wedding

The henna artist pulls my arm and begins her magic: applying henna to my hands. There are people everywhere, constantly pouring in and out of my home. I sit on my rocking chair, not ready to give it up just yet.

'Arey *dulhan*, lovely bride, stop moving, it will spoil the pattern,' the henna artist reprimands holding my hand tighter still. She begins drawing from the centre of my palm, working her way outwards, slowly building an intricate pattern, unique and visually beautiful, little flowers, leaves, paisleys, tiny hearts and dots all woven together with lines and crescents dipped in hopes of consummating unrealized dreams. She asks, 'Do you want to take off your ring so I can apply henna. I like hands to mirror each other and if you wear your ring, it will leave a little gap.'

'No, a little imperfection is just about perfect. I'll risk both the hands looking a little different,' I reply.

Perfection is not the call of the hour in the application of a temporary henna tattoo for it will fade in time taking its imperfection with it. I decide to keep wearing my engagement ring and she insists no more, focusing on her task at hand, literally. I gaze at my left hand, my shy pampered skin peeks from under the delicate and elaborate pattern of henna. It appears entirely feminine and traditionally bridal. I smile thinking of my chubby self from a dozen years ago. A vivid memory of me standing at the henna ceremony of Colonel Elahi's daughter—a memory, it appears, from another lifetime.

I was almost a young teen attending the traditional henna ceremony a day before the wedding. The rather large affair was being held at the Sea View Apartments by the Arabian Sea. The flat was perfect for a family of five and housed four bedrooms, but certainly not fit for a party of over two-hundred people dressed in their finest clothes and ornate gold jewellery. It was an autumn wedding, fun to dress up for, but not ideal to attend with bodies so many and space so little.

I remember standing under the archway dividing the drawing room and the dining room, pinned to a wall watching and singing enthusiastically. The two large rooms could have been an advertisement for a product named *pretty young girls galore*, if ever there was a product like that. A pretty girl played the dholak while another tapped it with a spoon, and a third beat the tambourine. The three worked the beat in rhythmic union creating a musical tempo that played a dynamic background to the singing and the clapping girls surrounding the trio.

They sat on thick floor carpets, covered with *chandni* and merged one wedding song into another, a tradition synonymous with South Asian weddings. Each song was more romantic than the last; some playful, some laced in romance and teasing the bride and groom about their much awaited enchanting togetherness, some focused on the melancholy of an impending emptying nest for the parents of the bride, some featuring the beauty of the bride and vigour of the groom. But my forever favourite wedding song was the bittersweet 'Ambwa Tale' by Amir Khusro. It's a centuries-old ballad laced in the welcome of the bridal palanquin, set under the shade of the large mango tree in the porch of the bride's father's home. The bride sings the song, bidding adieu to girlhood and doting parents, as she enters the bonds of a new relationship with her groom. The song is a shy rendition of virginal love, romantically hopeful and quintessentially sub-continental.

> *Ambwa tale ḍola rakh de niharwa,*
> *Aayi saawan ki bahaar re,*
> *Saiyaan ke aaye kahaar re.*

There was clapping, laughing, whistling, dancing, song, youth and merriment, and amidst the celebration appeared the bride wearing plain yellow, sans make-up and with a dupatta loosely draped over her head. She was a vision, glowing beautiful skin, demure look and shy eyes, almost ethereal and wearing her innocence to perfection. I gazed at her wondering how a girl in sunflower yellow sans other paraphernalia could be so intensely mesmerizing when compared to the decked girls surrounding her.

Today I have my answer.

It's the shy apprehension of entering a sensuous relationship and revelling in that very realization, the awareness of a girl's journey into becoming a woman, and the celebratory feast and fuss to mark the blessed union.

I snap out of my reverie as the henna artist gives me instructions on glazing my henna-laden hands and feet with oil, sugar water and lemon, to attain optimum colour, 'Dulhan, the darker the colour of the henna in the morning, after you wash it off, the more beautiful your relationship with your husband to be.'

The thought of a relationship has me wanting to stay in bed and indulge in more fantasy, a sudden tiredness overtaking me. 'Ayesha, snap out of your daydreams and go talk to Faiz, he just called for you,' announces Iffat in the middle of the verandah mayhem. There is pin-drop silence, momentarily, and then begin the expected catcalls, hooting, clapping, high-fiving amongst the people of the verandah.

'We are not hooting because he wants to talk to you, but are curious as to what is it that he wants to talk to you about just a few days before the wedding,' quips Sofia as she high-fives a very amused Dadi.

'Maybe he's changed his mind and doesn't want to marry her anymore, it's happened before you know,' says Sameer, draped on the newly upholstered cane sofa. Sofia throws a peeled orange at him from across the room, wanting to chide him for his remark, but instead he catches it like a professional wicket keeper and throws it in his mouth, saying, 'Thanks for peeling that orange. I was dying to eat one, but wasn't in the mood to peel it.'

And just like that an orange throwing contest begins as I escape to my room to speak to him.

≈

She felt numb with disbelief, there was deafening noise in her head, and in the deep recesses of the noise was a whisper, almost a repetitive echo of, *he's not coming.*

'But he must,' she whispered. Her eyes were hollow, voice flat. She sat at the edge of her bed staring at the dresser in the corner of her room. It was in complete disarray, much like her body, spirit and soul. Her hairbrush was on the floor, as always, and there were dozens of scattered bobby pins surrounding it. The eyeliner, lipsticks, face powder, all sat undisturbed and ready and waiting to be used. She walked to the mirror, picked up the darkest lipstick on the table and applied it to her pale lips, and then viciously rubbed it, taking off the freshly applied henna with it.

Her face was smeared with henna, she wiped it clean and reapplied the red lipstick. Crimson was her favourite colour, but her mother discouraged her from wearing it, insisting, *red is the colour for brides to be, or married women. Virgins must avoid red.*

Little did her mother know, or maybe she did?

She started laughing.

Her laughter was amplified, she laughed viciously, menacingly, and gradually the sound died turning to a low howl of a dying animal in severe pain. It became softer, finally choking itself to death.

She lay on the floor until day become night and night became day again. The rising sun championed her to prevail, to carry her baggage and rest at another destination. She got up, washed her face with cold water and felt a sudden wave of nausea in her throat, realizing she had not eaten in over twenty-four hours.

She looked in the mirror and found a reflection of a ghost, deathly pale, skin sallow, eyes hollow, lips quivering and bleeding red. She glanced at her hands, the colour of her henna tattooed hands was jaundiced orange, faded, forgotten and betrayed.

She sat down on the floor and felt nauseous again.

She wretched doubling over as her insides spewed saliva and spit, removing all doubt of living in sin.

She grabbed a towel, wiped her mouth, and walked to the plate of naan khatai sitting on her bedside table, smiling just a little. Despite the pathos of the moment, the sweetness of naan khatai calmed her soul a little, and smiling, she remembered Sharmeena's words: *Naan khatai never disappoints even when the rest of the world does.*

She chowed on the biscuit washing it down with water and instantly felt relief. It was time to weigh her options, but there was only one choice, a choice that would make her cousin, Khusro, blissfully happy. Slowly she paced to the door of her room, unlocked it, calmly walked into her mother's room and told the family that she would willingly marry Khusro. Then Shireen looked at her hands and said, 'I want to reapply the henna: Maybe next time the colour will be deeper.'

She never did.

꩜

I turn my head to the right and catch Faiz gazing at me, his face a few inches away from mine. He maintains a steady focus on my face, his eyes amused and suddenly he leans forward and says, 'Hey!'

I inch back some, laugh loud and spontaneous, replying, 'Hey back!'

We sit on a red carpet, speckled with maroon, green and yellow floor pillows, encased in rich velvet; a spread of flavoured hookah, hot chai, and a celebratory evening.

It's a glorious Karachi autumn night and the musical evening hosted by Faiz's family is set to begin soon. Faiz's garden makes for a beautiful venue. It's lush, green and infused with yellow fairy lights. Family and friends abound in celebrating this joyous occasion with us, I see Sofia standing with Ya Bhai, her body language coy, she throws her head back and laughs, leans into him and brushes something off his sleeve. I say a silent prayer for him and hope that he walks out unscathed from whatever Sofia's head is brewing.

With the wedding two days away and me wearing the proverbial sunflower yellow, it was impossible to convince Ammi to let me attend tonight's event until Faiz's mother called and requested her. Maintaining obligatory lihaaz, or consideration of sorts, Ammi gave in, and here I am enjoying what happens to be my beautiful wedding.

'Who let the two of you sit together? Is there no shame left in this godforsaken world?' interrupts Zaid with pretend horror and further asks, 'Are you two married? Not yet. Here, let me sit between the both of you. I look like Faiz, you want to marry me instead. It's happened before. One of our ancestors was meant to marry Mughal Emperor Babur's cousin, but instead ended marrying his own older brother's wife, or was it widow? I forget, but just in case you change your mind, I made a sherwani too.'

I laugh and vehemently say, 'Not this time!'

~

I feel a tap on my shoulder and see Farhad Mamu, his arms wide open. He arrived this afternoon from England and is staying at Salma Khala's house. I could have sworn he was wearing a charcoal grey suit when I saw him greeting my parents a few minutes earlier. Maybe my eyes are playing tricks?

'This hug is from your Nani, it's amazing how much you look like her. I remember her as you are today, but only fleetingly. Her youth was so short-lived. Once depression and obesity took over, it was as good as gone.' No one ever talks about my Nani, and this short exchange is a rarity of sorts.

'She died of depression and obesity?' I ask rhetorically.

'No, heartbreak!'

'Heartbreak? Who dies of heartbreak? Is that why you never got married?' I ask, hoping to get a straight answer.

'I don't know why I never got married. Maybe I'm paying the price for somebody else's sins. Sins of the father,' says Mamu pensively.

He looks so different from my Nana. His strikingly Persian looks are the opposite of my Nana's dark and angular southern-Punjabi appearance. In my mind's eye I can see him as a baby, and now understand why Nani named him Farhad, because he looks like a Persian lover.

I smile to myself wondering why she didn't name him Khusro?

Since my Nana's name was Khusro, and both men, namely Khusro and Farhad, were in love with doomed Shireen as told to us in the Persian mythological epic poem *Shahnamah*.

What made her choose the name Farhad over Khusro?

I'll never know.

Dadi is sitting on a sofa a few feet away from me and sends me a flying kiss, I laugh and send a flying kiss back to her and think about our conversation on the verandah from earlier today. She philosophized the wisdom of abstinence before marriage and it being the backbone of the survival of the institution of marriage in Eastern culture. She talked about her first time and how being in love, and the anticipation of the first time made it the most sacred night of her life. When she caught me smiling, she laughed and said, 'I was once young too. You now see a frail old body, but remember that I've been as old as you, and in love. Things were very different in our times, and though we did not have the liberties that your generation does, yet when a well-suited match was solemnized in marriage our sparks were as magical as any. The romance of a glance, an accidental touch, a subtle gesture is meaningful, almost mystical, and when a bond is being built and chemistry is felt on both sides it's best to prolong the yearning until after the wedding. The union then becomes an almost religious experience, and the bond stronger. Why do you think there are lesser divorces in our society? It's not because women are oppressed as the West would like you to believe, but because of the sanctity of marriage and the value of a virginal bed, virtue and patience.

'In life there is an order to things,' she continued. 'Rivers naturally flow downstream, the sun must set before it rises, death can only happen if there is birth, for a plant to grow a seed must be planted, and in a civil society marriage must happen before consummation of a marriage. Modern times encourage people to indulge in promiscuity, but that is not wise, it has never been wise. I understand, and to an extent also encourage a little liberty between a betrothed couple, but nothing of much consequence should occur between a couple before marriage.'

'Dadi, you are a bonafide rock star, and I'm your biggest fan.'

It's time to let go of my rocking chair, and my verandah too.

∾

She stood as if she were paralysed. The bride and the man sitting next to her took the wind out of Sharmeena. She blinked a few times convinced that her mind was playing tricks and stood in the doorway for a while.

The bride was almost Shireen from half a century ago.

Sharmeena wanted to move, but her feet felt like lead, as if cemented to the ground, and then she heard Mehreen's voice, 'Bari Phuppo, are you okay? Let's go sit down, the *mehfil-e-ghazal* is about to begin.'

She held Mehreen's hand and asked, 'Who's that man with the bride?'

'Oh, that's Ayesha's Mamu. Doesn't he look a lot like Dada? They could be twins a few decades apart. His name is Farhad too, what are the chances of that ever happening? Doppelganger with the same name, and settled in London too. If that's not a coincidence, what is?'

In life there are no coincidences, Sharmeena almost said, and then refrained not wanting to infer a connection to half a century ago.

'Has your Dada met him?' Sharmeena asked in a deadpan voice, not giving away the turmoil she felt. She eyed her brother, wearing a charcoal grey suit and standing some distance away.

'I don't think so. Have you met Ayesha? Let me introduce you to her, come,' Mehreen said, urging Sharmeena to move from the doorway. Just then the incomparable Sufi singer started her rendition of Amir Khusro's 'Rung' and Sharmeena felt a wave of pathos.

Fifty years too late, or is it? She questioned the silence confronting her.

A flood of memories washed over her as she remembered another time when Amir Khusro's poetry had induced similar emotion. In the end it was Farhad's lust that won, while Khusro's unrequited love disintegrated into a breathless death.

She walked to the drawing room, shut the door behind her and peeled the end of the curtain, soaking in the sights and sounds of the wedding. The Sufi singer's back was to her, and Ayesha and Faiz sat facing the singer at a distance.

If Farhad had married Shireen, things would have been different, much different.

There would be no Faiz, or Ayesha.

She peeked at the young couple again, and invariably smiled at the delightful picture they made. Ayesha, ethereal in bridal yellow, lost in thought and sitting with her knees to her chest with her arms wrapped around them; Faiz in a traditional white kameez-shalwar, and leaning into a large cylindrical floor pillow behind his bride, forming an almost crescent around her as the Sufi singer spun her magically mystical rendition of the passionate, romantic and timeless love ballad, the incomparable 'Rung'.

Sharmeena sighed, shook her head and pondered the aura of time. Maybe time is the ultimate strategist, creating new illusions, engineering intricate labyrinths, mixing them with old and time-tested mechanics, weaving them together and then finally placing humans into a puzzle. Maybe we are not meant to figure out the puzzle, but are only meant to create building blocks in the puzzle with our choices for the next generation, she thought.

She watched Faiz as he leaned into his bride to be, and moved a few inches behind her. Ayesha almost had her back to him and if she leaned back she could almost be resting on his chest. Remembrance and regret, that's what Sharmeena felt, a wave of nostalgia washed her senses and she wished she had followed Shireen's rushed decision of marrying a cousin. Maybe her intervention could have resulted in a legitimate outcome.

She wondered at the ways of fate, time, and the lessons people are meant to learn from them. Carrying Shireen's thought she walked out of the drawing room and decided to introduce herself. Habitually her nose followed the fragrance of the glorious homemade pulao made from the recipe Shireen had shared decades ago. There it was, glistening grand on Tuesday night, sitting high on a table a few feet away from the groom and his bride, and she smiled as she saw Ayesha reach for it, bringing life full circle on the wings of feast, time and poetry. **Tuesdays with pulao, welcome home, once again.**

Some call it kismet, some call it fate,
Some call it Samsara, it's the sweetest bait,
The stories of passion are as old as time,
Feast an enchanting vessel, delightfully sublime.

～

PULAO

The elite cooking of Pakistan and India expresses its central Asian, Turkish, Afghan and Persian roots, but we cannot ignore that its nourishment and beauty was epitomized because of spices, cultures and races indigenous to the region and land of the Indus. Sub-continental food is unique and has evolved over centuries to become what it is today, rich, vibrant, flavourful and elegant, like its people.

The surviving pulao recipes as relayed in books written by scholars from centuries past suggest the use of very few spices, the four whole garam masalas, ghee, coriander, cumin, fennel seeds, onions, ginger and garlic. But the real oomph came from preparing the goat, sheep or chicken yakhni (meat stock), and then straining it through mulmul cloth, and cooking the rice in the deliciously subtle stock. Once the rice was almost fluffed in the broth, the pot was sealed shut and steam cooking was initiated until completion.

The earliest mention of a dish named pilaf can be found in the transcripts of the history of Alexander the Great. It is believed that the young Greek conqueror enjoyed the reception he received at the hands of the locals of Bactria. The military forces accompanying him savoured the Bactrian dish of rice and meat, and took the recipe back with them to Greece and voila, we have the Mediterranean Pilaf.

Pilaf's arrival in Greece initiated its spread to Eastern Europe and entrenched itself permanently into most cuisines of the ancient world.

Ingredients

2 ½ lb mutton, small pieces (preferably goat leg or shoulder meat)

1 ½ tbsp fennel seeds

3 tbsp coriander seeds

2 large onions

1 tsp garam masala powder

1 tsp cumin

¼ to ½ cup oil

8 ½ mugs water

2 mugs rice

Salt to taste

1 ½ tbsp yogurt

1 tsp fresh ginger (chopped)

1 tsp fresh garlic (chopped)

Method

Slice one large onion in four quarters, add mutton, coriander seeds, fennel seeds, salt to taste and water. Bring to a boil and reduce heat to medium until mutton is cooked and the yakhni is reduced to half its original quantity (4 ¼ mugs).

Remove mutton pieces from stock (yakhni), and strain stock thoroughly through sieve, discarding the drained fennel, coriander and onions.

Pour oil and brown sliced onions into a large pot. Once the onions are golden brown add mutton, ginger, garlic, garam masala, cumin, salt to taste and yogurt. Stir on high heat for a few minutes adding mutton stock and bringing to a boil still on high heat; add pre-washed rice once stock comes to a boil.

Maintain high heat until the rice fluffs and the stock is a thin layer on the top. Set heat to low and seal the pot initiating the dum method (steam cooking after sealing the pot). Leave on low heat for 30 minutes, and your perfect pulao is ready to be enjoyed.

Beetroot (chukunder) Raita

Take two beets, discarding the stems. Boil until cooked. Remove from water, peel and julienne. In a bowl whisk 2 to 2½ mugs yogurt, add ½ cup washed and chopped onions, salt, a pinch of black pepper, 2 chopped green chillies, add the beets, sprinkle with chopped mint and cilantro and serve with pulao.

◆

NAAN KHATAI

Naan khatai is the quintessential desi biscuit and I can easily devour half a dozen in one sitting, and coupled with a hot cup of tea there is no better indulgence. It never disappoints.

Growing up in Karachi, a daily trip to Crispo Bakery was a must.

Bread, eggs and papay were bought fresh daily, unlike pantry hoarding in the West. And then there were many a days when a special treat of naan khatai, zeera biscuit or patties snuck itself into the bakery shopping. The effervescence of cardamom and pistachio combined with fresh baked flour and butter, roamed the house drawing all occupants to the lounge for naan khatai indulgence and more.

When it was time for me to make naan khatai, I obviously wanted to make them closest to the taste of Pakistani or North Indian naan khatai, infused with cardamom and pistachio. Needless to say, I was successful, and the outcome was absolutely delicious.

Ingredients

¼ cup semolina (sooji)
¾ cup unsalted butter
1 ¼ cup flour
½ cup and 1 tbsp of powder sugar
1 tsp vanilla
½ tsp to ¾ tsp cardamom powder
2 tbsp crushed pistachio or almonds (I prefer pistachio for it gives a very authentic taste)
1 egg yolk

Method (makes 10 to 12)

Sieve flour, add sugar, semolina and softened butter, and mix the ingredients well. Add vanilla, cardamom, pistachio into the dough, knead, it makes for a soft crumbly dough. Divide into 12 equal portions, forming little dough balls and use hands to press into a flattened little biscuit-shaped disc.

Refrigerate discs for 40 to 50 minutes. Remove, brush top with egg yolk, and set in oven, pre-heated at 350°C, for 12 to 15 minutes. Remove promptly (they will be soft when removed from oven but will completely harden once entirely cool), and set on wire rack to cool. Once cool, store in an airtight jar. Enjoy with a cup of garam garam chai.

◆

SHAHI KORMA

There is no better curry in the world than a korma cooked right. My personal favourite is the non-cream based korma; the authentic dahi-based meat curry infused with the royal aroma of cardamom, bay leaves and kewra water. My first memory of enjoying korma was at a wedding back home in Karachi, my lovely city by the sea. It was a biradari wedding, a distant cousin was getting married at the KMC sports complex and the two attractions at the happy union were the bride and the shahi deghi (royal) korma. I can almost taste it, the thick flavourful mutton curry wrapped in sheermal (a tortilla made of flour, milk, egg and ghee), and as the bite made the short journey from the plate to the mouth aided by the right hand, the left hand was busy picking up the cold-drink—a common term referring to soft drinks and soda in the desi realm—to dampen the taste of the delicious yet very spicy korma. Yes, the eyes and nose may have been watering, as they generally do of young ones when eating something spicy, but with a handy tissue and a drink in hand all seemed to be under control.

Korma literally means braising the meat, and the method for cooking korma was initial braising of meat in ghee, yogurt and spices and then simmering it in water to completion; blanched and finely ground nuts were also used as thickening agents. The Kashmiri roghan josh is a variation of the korma, as is the do piaza.

The four most popular korma curries in the subcontinent are Mughlai, shahi, Kashmiri and South Indian. The shahi and Mughlai are similar to the conventional korma recipe where yogurt is blended with almonds, and the meat is braised in yogurt, onions and spices and is later simmered. Once cooked, shahi korma is laced with malai (heavy cream), a Punjabi favourite, while the Mughlai korma is cooked with khoya right before being taken off the fire. The base for the South Indian korma is made of coconut milk and grated fresh coconut. This changes the taste of the korma entirely and gives it a uniquely delicious flavour, different from the korma enjoyed in Pakistan and North India.

Needless to say, the caramelized onion korma, whichever region it hails from, vegetarian or meat based, Mughlai or shahi, is an all-time subcontinental favourite. When it was time for me to make the delightful korma I looked at my own recipe book, and today I share my own recipe with you. No extra garnishes, achar or chutney required; with hot naan or shermaal your royal korma dinner is ready to be served.

Ingredients (serves 6 to 8)

6 to 8 oz oil
3 lb mutton or chicken
1 tsp heaped finely chopped fresh ginger
1 tsp heaped finely chopped fresh garlic
3 medium sized onions (finely sliced)
2 or 3 cinnamon sticks
½ tsp cloves
½ tsp black peppercorns
2 or 3 black cardamom pods
14 to 16 green cardamom pods, split
4 bay leaves
2 tbsp kewra water
2 to 3 tbsp almonds (optional)
Salt to taste

2 tsp red chilli powder

1 ½ tsp coriander powder

½ tsp garam masala powder

1 ½ tsp cumin powder

12 oz yogurt

56 to 64 oz water if cooking mutton; 40 to 48 oz water if cooking chicken

Method

Heat oil, fry onions until golden brown, drain onions and set aside.

In the same oil fry whole garam masalas (cinnamon, cloves, and peppercorn) and green cardamom for a couple of minutes, adding meat. Fry at high heat, adding the chopped ginger-garlic, yogurt, powdered masalas, salt and fried onions. Braise meat for 10 to 15 minutes, stirring constantly.

Bring water to a boil and add to meat. Let the korma boil for a few minutes before lowering the heat to medium. Let cook, adding bay leaves and kewra water. Once curry thickens, meat becomes tender and oil separates, your korma is ready to be served.

Optional: Garnish with fried almonds once korma is cooked, or add blanched almonds to korma 15 minutes before taking off fire.

Acknowledgements

Amna Tirmizi Naqvi—sisterhood, the next best thing to motherhood.

Musti and Ali Naqvi—brothers were made to not let you fall.

Amber Azam Kureshi and Amna Mumtaz—best friends were made to understand when no one else does.

Aneeqa Nawaz Akhtar—thank you for taking this journey with me.

Sophia Akhtar—thank you for representing my younger audience.

Aisha Zaidi—thank you for your sound advice, and for always seeing the bright side.

Zubeida Mustafa—thank you for being my mentor, guide and an inspiration for more than a quarter century.

Late Musadiq Sanwal, editor dawn.com—thank you for understanding my passion for storytelling, and food anthropology.

Shalini Shehkar—thank you for letting my imagination take flight.

Elina Majumdar—thank you for your guidance and sound support.

Rinita Banerjee—thank you for making it easy, and for listening when it mattered most.

My three kids—thank you for giving me motherhood, and the sweet madness accompanying it.

Rupa Publications—thank you for being the best publisher a writer can ask for.

Fawad Ahmed—thank you for being the fuel to my flame.

Glossary

Kinship terms

Dada—Paternal grandfather

Dadi—Paternal grandmother

Chacha—Father's younger brother

Khala—Mother's sister

Lala—Older brother in Phusto, a language spoken by Pathans

Phuppo—Father's sister

Mami—Wife of mother's brother

Tayajee—Father's older brother

Terms related to food items, recipes and methods of cooking

Ajwain—Carom seeds

berian—A Persian word that refers to the process of frying before cooking. In the original method of cooking biryani (in Persia), the rice was fried before the dum method.

besan—Chickpea or gram flour

garam masala—A blend of specific spices either added whole or ground, for aroma and flavour

daal—Lentil

dahi—Yogurt

kewra—Known as 'thandai' in India, this is a transparent liquid extracted from pandanus flowers; usually used for flavouring dishes.

ghee—Clarified butter

khoya—Unsweetened condensed milk

Khichdi—A rice, vegetable and lentil dish

Mutanjan—A mughlai dish that has not survived the test of time. It was referred to as biryani mutanjana and pulao mutanjana. This is made with rice, ghee, spices, sweet meats, khoya, nuts, sugar, salt and meat. The authentic mutanjan is not a popular dish, but people usually combine savoury pulao with zarda, and spicy biryani with zarda, and refer to it as mutanjan.

papay—Tea rusk in Urdu

sajji—A Balouchi specialty, where rice-stuffed whole lamb, or whole chicken, marinated in salt and green papaya is cooked on an open flame on skewers.

Thadal—Almond milk laced with poppy seeds, melon seeds and green cardamom

Other terms

azaan—Muslim call to prayer

baadshahi—Royal

baraat—Wedding procession

biradari—Clan

chandi aur sonay kay warq—Silver and gold leaves

chandni—White, crisp cotton sheets spread on top of carpets and rugs at ceremonies, where an event requires floor seating. It can also mean moonlight in Urdu.

charbagh—Four gardens

dasterkhwan—Urdu for table cloth or great spread

dhamaal—Musical subgenre (dance) on *qawali*; could also mean the beat from the dhol and tabla

dhol—Small drum, folk musical instrument

diya—Oil lamp

dulhan—Bride

fateha—Prayer

galli—Alley

jharoka—Enclosed hanging balcony

khatta—sour

langar—Free food served to all as community service

luddi—Punjabi folk dance

makbara—Mausoleum

mazaar—Shrine

mehfilain—Intimate gathering involving music and dance; *mehfilain* is plural of *mehfil*

mehfil-e-ghazal—Musical evening; ghazal is a lyric poem with a repeated rhyme, typically on the theme of love, normally set to music.

mehfil-e-sema—Spiritual gatherings

mureed—Committed one

nikaah—Marriage contract

nikaahkawan—The one who reads the Muslim marriage contract, pronouncing the marriage as legal

payal—Anklet

qawaal—One who sings the *qawali*

qawaali—Sufi devotional song/music

qurbani ka bakra—Sacrificial goat/lamb

ralli—Traditional quilt from Sindh

sema—The Turkish dance ritual with whirling dervishes

shahi hamam—Royal bath

thevaar—Religious festival

zari, dubka, moti, sitaray—Gold thread, embroidery, pearls and sequence embellishments